Published in paperback, 2023, in associ.
JV Author Services
www.jvauthorservices.co.uk
jvpublishing@yahoo.com

ISBN:

Editing and cover by JV Author Services, 2023.
Cover photo by SkyBlueSophie – www.skybluesophie.co.uk

Dedication

To the Gibbons family, who provided funding to make this project possible, and to the Writing for Pleasure Group members whose amazing talent is showcased within.

In Memory of David Murray
10/05/1937 – 28/07/ 2023
Rest in Peace
We will miss your punchy, gritty anecdotes and stories

Introduction

By Pauline Bennett

When Anne Gibbons died, a light in Saltburn u3a went out. Anne was a lively member of several groups and loved the Creative Writing group. We would like to invite you to step into this little anthology we have put together in a tribute to Anne.

Here you will find all manner of delights, poems, and stories, interlaced with a few facts about Anne and of course, her beloved 'doggy tales'.

Come for a stroll through Anne's life as told by herself, her brother, and the u3a Writing for Pleasure group.

Memories of Anne Gibbons

By Karin Slade

Anne was one of six children, being number five of the family, and she used to rattle their names off at speed – Joe, Agnes, Tessa, Jerry, Anne, and Jim.

Anne stayed on at school to take the School Certification examinations, which preceded GCEs, and left school with good results but no particular direction in mind.

Had she been able to continue, she might have studied to become a teacher. However, she felt her parents would prefer her to start work. With two brothers and two sisters older than her and one brother younger, she understood and felt lucky to have been able to stay past the fourteen-plus school leaving age.

*****

Haiku
Anita Langham

Through red nostril, ox
blows a blast of summer grass,
on sweet cloud, gnat soars

Memories of Anne Gibbons

By Karin Slade

Anne was closest to her younger brother Jim and, bonded by their wartime experiences, they were in regular contact. Anne never quite understood why Jim should choose to reside in the Isle of Wight when the lovely Teesside was on offer.

*****

Haiku
Anita Langham

Breeze sighs in tree-like
winter sea, or wingbeats of
a million starlings

Anne

By Jim Gibbons (Anne's Brother)

I crashed upon this alien land at birth,
A Martian shipwrecked on a nightmare earth.

Begun in torture, raised in a time of strife,
Fearful of death and terrified of life,
Baffled by people, much perplexed by things,
And slow to learn the skills that living brings.

But you my sister, confident and bold,
From your Olympian heights of three years old
Resolving to this scrap a hand to lend
Became my guide, philosopher, and always, friend.

Storm Over Huntcliff

By Meg Fishburn

Do you ever walk along Huntcliff
On a January day?
Wild claws of hail snatch at your face,
And the devil's dark clouds play
Above Huntcliff's brooding brow.

Long gone now is Skylark's rise,
The curlew's haunting call.
Replaced by pluming wind-whipped spray,
While through the drenching hail
Walk the ghosts of yesterday.

Did you see the maid from long ago,
Turn your head from her sightless stare?
Hear lookout's call for arms to protect
The cliff land held so fair?
The mighty cliff, relentless, stands firm.

Here now, the cries of the sailor,
Through north wind's deathly moan.
The smugglers watch with greed-filled eyes
As their bounty washes home
Beneath Huntcliff's pitiless glare.
Ice fingers shred the webs
That laced once yellow gorse.
Torn ankles, as you stumble
Through the crazed gale's endless force.
Huntcliff, unmoved, looks on.

The Face at the Window

By Pauline Bennett

There it was again, a face, a human face but almost impossible to distinguish age or gender from this angle. But at least Jo knew she had not imagined it. The window in question was one of those Velux windows set at an angle over what she always supposed was the kitchen of the house. That was the third time she had seen it. How strange, but of course, as soon as she started down her stairs, real life crowded out the mysterious face until later one afternoon.

Jo was a teacher in a local primary school but today she had been on a course which had finished early. Not being required to report back to school, she had come home slightly earlier than usual, and now, changing out of her more formal clothes, she glanced out of her bedroom window and there it was again. The face. The light was different at this time of day and she could see clearly that it was a small child's face, possibly a girl as it had quite long, dark curls framing a little oval face. She waved. At first, there was no reaction from the child but then a small fist was raised, and slowly unfurled fingers became a waving hand. Then it disappeared. Jo waited for some time but there was no further appearance. Niggly worries began to infiltrate her thoughts. She had never seen a child at that house, ever. The only occupant seemed to be a late middle-aged man and his wife, who were both sombre and reclusive. The man occasionally ventured out in a rather ancient blue car but Jo had only ever seen the woman on a Sunday morning when it appeared she might have been attending a church service. Even then, a politely called 'good morning' from Jo was never reciprocated. Jo decided that she would watch the house for the next half hour, particularly as the car was missing from the driveway. But to no avail, no face, no little wave, and no sign of life, yet she knew she had not imagined it. Perhaps she should talk to one of the other neighbours but then again they were all out at work like she was. Nevertheless, Jo decided to try and make enquiries until the next day when the whole mystery took yet another turn.

Around 5 am, Jo was woken by the insistent flashing of blue

lights through her thin curtains. Just the lights – no sound, no sirens. Peering sleepily threw a chink in the voile, she saw an ambulance on the driveway and two paramedics hastily making their way laden with equipment to the side door which doubled as the main entrance. Almost holding her breath, Jo wondered who might be needing an ambulance when after about ten minutes, one of the paramedics carefully extracted the chair device they used to transport patients and sure enough, returned with the man, his head slumped on his chest and an IV line being held aloft by the other paramedic. He was quickly followed by the woman who had dressed in a hurry with feet still clad in furry slippers. She was clutching a bag and pulled the door to, and ran to the back doors of the ambulance. Jo could see quite clearly that the door had not shut, caught on some thick curtain or similar. So, this was her chance. The ambulance reversed off the drive and now, with its sirens accompanying the blue light, sped out of the small cul-de-sac.

Quickly donning jeans and a thick jumper, Jo ran silently across the street and pushed open the door. The place was in disarray. The man had collapsed down the stairs carrying a tray, the contents of which were all over the floor. A cat wound its tail around her legs and mewed hopefully, but Jo was on a mission. She had to find the little face. A quick search of the various rooms produced nothing, no child, no clothing or bed suitable for a child. Nothing. But she knew what she had seen, so began hunting for keys and her luck was in. A very neat key rack with keys all carefully labelled. Grabbing them all and following the labels, a quick search again produced nothing until there was a little cry. Only a little one which seemed to be stifled but unmistakably came from behind an old-fashioned kitchen unit. Opening the door of the unit, Jo almost jumped for joy. There behind the curtain of sorts was a door. But which key? Unable to find one that fitted amongst the bunch in her fist, she began to knock on the door gently and call out. At first, nothing but then two voices and some shuffling, and then her eyes alighted on a small jar near the light switch and sure enough, a small Yale key that fitted perfectly. Speaking softly so as not to alarm whoever was behind the door, Jo turned the key and was frustrated again. The door did not yield. Turning away quickly, her jumper caught on the key, and to her amazement, the door pulled open. A strong odour of unkempt bodies and stale food swept across her but when she peered into the gloom beyond the door, she could not believe her eyes. Not one little face but two, possibly twins, and behind them, the face of a teenage girl with tears streaming down her face.

Memories of Anne Gibbons

By Karin Slade

On most days Anne could be found in what I referred to as her 'nest', more commonly known as a sofa but tucked around her were piles of books, old diaries, copies of the Gazette (turned either to the crossword page or the death notices), letters and newspaper clippings from her brother, copies of the Catholic Church magazine, quite a few pop socks, copies of the Radio Times and Gardeners World, several pens and notepads with creative writing 'homework' and on the coffee table mugs of green tea – ordinary tea occasionally but never ever, ever coffee!

*****

Haiku
Anita Langham

Row of bricks where
hooves scrabble for purchase
steep donkey path

Ode to the Giant Racer

By Norma Cuthbert

In days of yore, I have been told
The people of Redcar were very bold.
The pleasure they sought was beyond my comprehension
For I have never been that bold, with intention
From what I view when I reminisce
I'd chose to forget; I'd give it a miss.

Though the pleasures they sought were few and far
They knew no better so I'll give them a star!
Their bravery, I will admit,
For it is far beyond my remit.
My thanks I give great giant for your loss
For building my home, your death it cost.

GIANT RACER, PLEASURE PARK, REDCAR.   A. E. Graham, Photo., Redcar.

Shadows on the Stair

By Anita Langham

At five she sat on the very top stair
In winceyette knickers her mother made
Shielding her doll and hiding her face
From a huge cloud that looked like a bear.

Up and down, up and down,
Choosing a path on the staircase of time.

Heads side by side on a rising tread
She and her lover when she was twenty
Cuddles and kisses shared with the carpet
Dreams woven into each stitch and thread

Up and down, up and down,
Weaving a tale in the staircase of time.

At thirty, tewing with older son
Heavy with second child, she slipped,
Lay, hurting, straining ears to hear
The heartbeat of her unborn one.
Up and down, up and down,
Hopes and fears on the staircase of time.

At forty, yelling at teenagers up the stair
Get up, get washed, tidy those rooms,
Pass some exams, get a job, instead
Of stinking in bed without a care.

Up and down, up and down,
Fledging chicks off the staircase of time
Two grandsons and one granddaughter
Larked on the stairs when she was fifty.
Only the damage and stains remain now,
Along with the echoes of their laughter.

Up and down, up and down,
Wearing a groove in the staircase of time.

When she was sixty her husband died
Her life began when she married him
They carried him down with his best suit on,
She sat on the stairs for hours and cried
Up and down, up and down,
Bitter tears on the staircase of time.

Helped by her daughter up to bed
They had to keep stopping before the top.
'Those knees and you are over seventy –
You need a bungalow, Mum,' she said.

Up and down, up and down,
Hitting a rut in the staircase of time.

At eighty, peering up with failing sight
Up in space, back in time, glimpsing,
Half-remembered at the very top
A little patch of fading golden light.

Up and down, down and down,
Leaving a ghost on the staircase of time.

*****

Haiku
Anita Langham

Squatting in my mind
this stone cold dark day winter,
hard as grounded toads

Memories of Anne Gibbons

By Karin Slade

Anne revelled in her natural pessimism, loving nothing better than having it challenged and always with a twinkle in her eye.
You knew when Anne was happy as she whistled.
She kept a diary every day and had over thirty volumes which she loved to dip into on a random basis.

*****

Haiku
Anita Langham

Yoke, silver-grey wood,
worn to glass by chafing bone
and muscle mountain

Delivery Delayed

By Michael Kirke

Extract from a novel about a National Trust Acorn Camp in which volunteer conservationists, aided by huntsmen and servicemen, foil rival gangs of animal smugglers.

The Lagoon

On arrival at the saltwater lagoon at the end of the Nabob's Dunes, the volunteers trooped to the spots marked by the National Trust coast warden as suitable landing places for waterfowl. Part of our job was to clear away vegetation from an area about three yards by three to make a gently sloping ramp similar to those found where cattle drink from fieldside streams. This was a quite simple matter of digging away at the miniature cliff-like edge to ease the passage of young waterfowl ashore to graze. The other job of removing invading water plants is no less simple although it encroaches on the mucky and off-putting as indicated by some of the volunteers.

"Oh, my God! It's filthy!" exclaimed Jackie, the tourism advisor, to be followed by a practical inquiry of, "I don't believe this. How deep is this stuff?" from the shy and scholarly Pete. "It's never as bad as it looks," commented Sandy displaying the technical expertise of the detached marine biologist from the safety of the bank.

"Ja. Is always vorse," said Jan, the Dutch police cadet who had done this before. "You never are knowing with the sea. Come, I show how." He plunged into the thigh-deep water followed by Marcus, eager to show that Yorkshiremen were as good as anyone. "Wow! That's not water!" he shouted gleefully, "That's liquid ice."

Jan then demonstrated the technique of standing in the glutinous ankle-deep mud, bending down so that the water all but reached his armpits as he grasped a handful of reeds. "Now is good holdings and slowly pullings. If not, the plants are breaking and backward fall into the water. This is vet arsings. Ja"

"Oh, Jan. I'd love to have you in court as a witness," quipped Jane, the legal secretary. "Can you imagine the beak asking 'Please define the technicalities of vet arsings for the jury?'"

In no time at all, each team had split into two groups, one clearing the landing place and the other quickly resembling the Papuan tribe whose warriors wear mud for war. As you may imagine, the sticky mud clung to the uprooted weeds with a lover's embrace while unwary workers who had pulled too hard in their eagerness went vet arsings to cheers from equally wet and filthy teammates.

"Hey, man. This is fun," hooted Liam together with Paolo, a caterer from Glasgow, with ghastly enthusiasm, before turning to Harry to ask, "And you marine biologists get paid for this? That's cool!"

"Too bloody cool," retorted Mark thinking of maintenance jobs in a wet pit. "Especially when you're a thousand feet down with no light except your headlamp."

"Sounds a tough number," commented Bill, the biker, "Me, I'll settle for a hot machine shop any day," before going on with, "Hey, you lot on the bank," he regarded the still clean workers shovelling away. "Time to change over. Come on in. The water's lovely. So's the muck!"

Democracy had its way as the teams changed over with their barely recognisable partners who offered derisive advice on how to get really wet and dirty. As it's no good leading this sort of show from a safe distance Martin and I 'mucked in' vet arsings with the best.

Can you think of a more suitable expression?

Memories of Anne Gibbons

Precis from Anne's autobiography

A career in nursing crossed Anne's mind, but nurse training did not commence until the age of eighteen.

A school friend mentioned an advertisement in The Evening Gazette for a new type of pre-nursing training at St Luke's Hospital for the mentally ill.

With little idea of how to care for these patients she, along with her friend Pat, applied and was accepted. September 1950 was the starting date.

*****

Haiku
Anita Langham

Sleepy seahorse nods
in soft moon circle. Still world,
silent, silver night

The Gardener

By Molly Griffin

It was the robin, balanced skilfully on the telephone wire which drew Elizabeth's attention. She watched its little head bob, and its black beady eyes seemed to be looking into her living room. It reminded her of the many times her Frank had worked in the garden, a robin somewhere in attendance. Perhaps it was the same robin. It was only six months since Frank had pottered about out there and since he had died so suddenly.

Throughout the following months, their garden had been neglected. Elizabeth had never even looked at it, had not even wheeled her chair around to see what her husband had lovingly cared for.

It was because of the robin then that Elizabeth wheeled herself to the window overlooking the back garden and whilst sadly seeing the untended, weed-filled flower beds, made up her mind to go out.

Even the thought of finding her jacket and of actually going out of the door again was a sort of adventure. The jacket was where the home help had hung it some time after Frank's funeral, and, with that more or less on and a scarf to guard against the April morning chill, she was ready.

After nearly six months, there she was sitting in her chair in the garden after having negotiated the shallow ramp from the back door. It was a long time since she had sniffed such fresh morning air. Its clarity and freshness made her feel so much more alive after the stale embrocation-laden atmosphere of her self-imposed imprisonment.

Years ago, Frank had made the raised flower beds for her. There was one centre rectangular-shaped one, with another two narrow beds along the brick walls. The third edge of the garden, on the side of the path which led to the gate, was formed by a hedge of currant bushes, unpruned from last year and almost flowering. Elizabeth could smell its faint cat odour. She smiled to herself, remembering how she had once cut sprays of its welcome early flowers, and Frank had sniffed around the room, blaming Georgie, their grey and white cat.

Slowly, Elizabeth manoeuvred the chair around the flower bed, stopping now and again to look all around, wanting to take in everything at once. Georgie appeared from one of his secret errands, his tail welcoming her. With delighted purring, he rubbed his body against the chair wheels. She was glad of his company as he eventually sat near her appearing to be examining the tangle of weeds with her. Elizabeth guessed that he probably revelled in its wildness, and, as if reading her thoughts, he left her to go and investigate an almost imperceptible quiver in the grass.

Having toured the perimeter of the centre bed twice, it dawned on Elizabeth that each corner had been very roughly tidied. The snowdrops which Frank had planted there had finished flowering, but their thin, weary-looking leaves were lying on fresh earth. She looked as closely as she could to make sure that there was certainly no doubt about it. It could be Sally, her home help. She did not like gardening and it would seem that she never had the time anyway. Elizabeth looked over at Georgie and laughingly said, "It wasn't you, was it, puss?"

Frank and she had always said he was clever, but surely not that clever!

Whoever it was had carefully dug the soil to allow the snowdrops to breathe and grow unhindered, yet in the centre, the roses were straggling, completely unpruned, and ignored. Elizabeth remembered Frank planting them on a wedding anniversary.

"All Elizabeth roses," he had said, showing her the delicate pink Elizabeth of Glamis and the pale yellow-pink Elizabeth Harkness.

She decided at once to see to them and then halted her wild plans, for how could she possibly cope? It was not easy from a wheelchair. Bending over, she caught at the length of goosegrass with the hook end of her stick and pulled. What looked like a very thin, green snake twisted in the air toward her. Its rough surface clung to her hand and sleeve until she shook it away and threw it onto the paved path. She captured other weeds within easy reach until there was a small heap.

Thoroughly bored by now, Georgie had stalked halfway back to the house as if implying that the day was turning cooler and that the trial visit had been long enough for a first time. Georgie's teatime must also be imminent, and that was even more important. Elizabeth followed, feeling pleased with what she had attempted on her own and yet still puzzled about the snowdrops.

The next days were disappointingly wet and cold, and the view from the window was not encouraging. It was late afternoon two days later when the rain stopped, the mist lifted, and weak sunshine lit up the rest of the day. Elizabeth moved the chair nearer to the window, enjoying the warmth, and she saw immediately the small figure of the paperboy standing by the rosebush. His bright fluorescent bag which usually dwarfed him, was hanging by its strap on the back gate. His attention was taken by the small pile of weeds left on the path. Elizabeth watched, keeping still, and saw the boy gather up the greenery and take it to a compost bin next to the small garden shed. Then, wiping his hands down his jeans, he walked all around the flower bed, unhooked his paper bag, let himself out of the gate, and disappeared down the road.

Frank and she had let the boy take a shortcut through their garden from front to back. It did not make the journey that much shorter, but the boy seemed to think that it did and so the habit formed. Elizabeth remembered how Frank would often have a word or two with him as he heaved his heavy bag along on one shoulder. Curly, he had said his name was, and there seemed to be no reason to suggest that there was another, with his tight, wiry curls atop his black face. Frank had said that Curly seemed to like someone to talk to because his face would split into a smile and he would stop to watch Frank gardening. Together they discussed football or school or even the quality of the many sweets that Curly was invariably chewing. Elizabeth hoped that folks were not in a hurry for their papers.

The next day, she had made up her mind to be in the garden when Curly came through. So, wheeling herself to the other side of the rose bed, she sat reading, enjoying the sun and Georgie's antics as he slyly eyed birds whilst pretending to be busy washing himself.

Suddenly, she heard the front gate click shut, the snap of the letterbox, and then the sound of feet coming along the side of the house to the back. Round the corner came Curly, eyes busy with a magazine meant for delivery.

With little cries of pleasure, Georgie left Elizabeth's side going to meet the boy, who looked every bit as pleased at the meeting. Georgie rolled over and over with joy at having someone tickle his tummy. Then, suddenly, for no apparent reason, he sprang up and ran across to Elizabeth as if wanting her to have a share of the welcome.

It was then that Curly saw Elizabeth. His face broke into a huge smile as he walked to the gate, hooking his bag over the side. Then he turned back towards Elizabeth, his eyes alight with pleasure.

"Now we can start gardening again properly," he said. "You and me'll soon have Frank's garden right."

He dived behind the shed and brought out Frank's very old and well-used trowel. Elizabeth watched as the boy set to work – paper round was forgotten for the time being. Georgie chased the weeds and pebbles as they were flung to the path and showed off with his acrobatic tumbles.

The sun warmed her, and after many lonely weeks, Elizabeth felt the slow return of contentment. It was indeed spring. A fresh start to the year. Life would be bearable again.

Memories of Anne Gibbons

By Karin Slade

Anne had a long career in nursing, starting as a 'pinky' at St Luke's Hospital in Middlesbrough when she was sixteen. This was a pre-nursing year and Anne remained friends with the other 'pinkies' throughout the remainder of her life.

Anne nursed in London and Sheffield before returning to her childhood home in Norton where she looked after her parents and at the same time, took up a post as a nurse tutor at St Luke's where her nursing career had begun.

There was one problem. What to do with her dog, Blackie? He would be left alone for long hours until her shift ended.

A solution arose, after speaking to the hall porter, she would take Blackie to work. To make an official request would surely be tied up in all sorts of red tape and possible rejection of her plan, so she made a brave decision to just take him there. She got away with it and Blackie became a much-loved addition to the hospital.

*****

Haiku
Anita Langham

Wind through trees
Whoosh of starlings
August sea

Memories of Anne Gibbons

Jim Gibbons, Anne's brother, has kindly permitted his poem to be included. After writing poetry during the war to amuse his colleagues, he re-visited the skill years later inspired by the fact his sister had acquired a dog. Blackie, he says, was a 'bitsa', bits of this and bits of that, but predominantly Manchester Terrier.

Odds and Ends

By Jim Gibbons

My mistress came to get me
When I was very young.
She greeted me with outstretched hand,
I answered with my tongue.

I liked her touch, I loved her voice,
Adored her very smell!
And I'm a lucky dog
Because she fell for me as well.

My mistress only has two legs,
She has no tail at all.
She cannot run as fast as I
And will not jump a wall.
We go out walking twice a day
And when I'm off my lead
I dash in all directions for
The exercise I need
My mistress follows on behind
At her sedated pace;
She loves the walks as much as I
But does not like to race.

I don't want her to get too fat

Or let fitness slack:
I played with her just throw the ball -
Then let her fetch it back!

Although she has no sense of smell
She gets a better view
Than I, because she's five feet five
And I am two foot two.

Once in the park and off my lead
There's nothing there can catch me:
No creature with my turn of speed,
No dog nor man can match me.
The dogs that follow me on foot,
The boys that go on wheels,
I toy with them, and when I've done
Show two clean pairs of heels.

Sally

Jim Gibbons

Shall I learn to love this lady?
After life-long blows and knocks?
Lick her hand when walking daily?
Let the tail go wagging gaily?
Yes!

Blackie's Epitaph

Goodbye, Black Dog,
Our love you truly earned.
Dark days were brightened
By your cheering touch.
We'd be a better species
If we learned
To ask so little
And give so much.

Photos

By David Hamilton

Yes it's me in the picture you see
The photo you hold in your hand,
I'm down on the beach on my grandmother's knee
Sat with my toes in the sand.

No, I don't look like that anymore
I know I look little, you're right,
That picture was taken a long time ago
When photos were all black and white.

But you know this seaside, you know this beach
We paddled right next to the pier,
You played with your sister while I got ice cream
It was in the summer of last year.

Where's Granny now? Gone long ago
I am now Granny to you,
You might have grandkids, you never know
And you might take photographs too.

Pictures with colour, pictures that move
Yellow and gold for the sun,
Photos remind us of people we love
And that way they're never gone.

Rocks become stones, stones become sand
Beaten together by waves,
The tide then retreats away from the land
Day after day after day.

Memories of Anne Gibbons

By Rita Beckham

Within the writing group, Anne enjoyed the challenge of the monthly topic, which we all did. Always before reading it out to the group she would say, 'It's a load of rubbish,' read it, then say again, 'It's rubbish.' It never was, in fact, it was quite entertaining. No one within the group ever criticised each other's work. It was always the best we could write at the time, therefore we were encouraged to write better. It was lovely to see individuals improve. We all appreciated the comradeship within the group.

*****

Haiku
Anita Langham

Octopus skin seeps
rainbows as she remembers
mermaid's lullaby

Russian Holiday 2006

By Anne Gibbons

Going to Russia was one of the many things that never crossed my mind, but the more I thought of it the more the idea appealed to me. It was to be a u3a holiday so very unusual, but at least with some people that I knew and the preparation in the form of an introduction to the language and culture given by a person who had taught Russian seemed a great opportunity.

So, at around 5.30 am on Friday, October 14th we were taken by minibus to Teesside Airport, then via Heathrow to Moscow, where we were met by Irina, who was to be our guide for three days. Irina was a fount of knowledge and very good at passing on her enthusiasm for her subjects and love of her country.

Our first morning was spent hopping in and out of the coach enjoying a tour of the city. We spent quite a long time in Red Square and were surprised to learn it had been entitled Red Square long before the socialist revolution as 'Red' means beautiful. It was indeed beautiful, particularly the impressive bright colours and the onion domes of the Cathedral of Saint Basil, which stood out splendidly against the blue sky, contrasting with the buildings of red brick.

Seeing the Kremlin, we learned that Kremlin means fortress and was used by citizens as a refuge in times of trouble. I was surprised to see not one, not two, but five churches within the Kremlin walls.

Then we visited the Cathedral of the Assumption or The Dormition Cathedral, the walls of which were covered in the most beautifully coloured frescoes. The iconostasis or screen, which in Orthodox churches separates the sanctuary from the body of the church was very impressive. Having seen children there I asked Irina what the church would mean to them as they would have been brought up with no knowledge of religion. She replied that the church had never died, just gone underground.

We followed this with a trip to the Metro for two very short trips of two stations each. This was to enable us to see the works of art that make up the Metro. Each station is differently decorated, some have statues of workers, others have a classical theme or just attractive frescoes but almost no advertising. The efficiency of the system intrigued me. The train stops for precisely forty-five seconds, and anybody who isn't on just has to wait for the next one which appears in a couple of minutes.

After dinner, we were eventually on our way to the train station for the overnight sleeper to St Petersburg. It was a new train, the Red Arrow, very smart in its décor and very well equipped. I had a double compartment to myself. On a little table was a selection of 'goodies' – biscuits, a roll and butter, cheese, a cake, a drink, etc. At six in the morning, the lady in charge of the carriage made me a large glass of Russian tea, and we arrived at St Petersburg station at a quarter to eight. We were welcomed on the platform by our new guide, Maria, and after breakfast at our new hotel, we embarked on a tour of the city as in Moscow. St Petersburg was built from scratch by Peter the Great, who had the swampy ground drained by canals and the buildings designed by French and Italian architects, hence its name, The Venice of the North. The buildings were lower and painted in pastel colours because the weather was often grey and dreary. It was a very spacious city with lots of open squares, public gardens, and very many trees, and is indeed a stunningly beautiful city.

The next day we visited the Hermitage, the famous museum containing all forms of art, which is housed in the Winter Palace. Inside it was opulent, with many gold decorations. One room was the 'Amber Room' with walls made almost entirely of amber, which was entirely looted by the Germans and reproduced later from photographs.

We had wanted to see a ballet while we were in Russia but on finding out that the seats would cost more than a hundred pounds, we chose a Cossack concert instead which was very colourful and lively. The following day we began our journey home.

Whilst in Russia, we discovered that the communist regime had only collapsed fifteen years previously and that both our guides had lived through very turbulent times. Irina told us she had grown up in a family of seven living in a large room in a communal apartment. She felt she had benefitted greatly from the excellent education system which was free right through school and university up to PhD level. After qualifying, they were then appointed to a job with little choice. After the fall of communism, there was an economic collapse. The people who suffered the most from the huge devaluation of the rouble were the old, whose life savings were virtually wiped out. Maria felt that old people were now in a worse position than under communism when at least they felt they were cared for and could pay their way. The few beggars we saw were old women. Irina pointed out that throughout the history of Russia, it has been a society of great extremes, as she said, they don't seem able to strike a happy medium. However, after our visit, I for one felt I had gained a great respect for their resilience in coping with the tremendous challenges life has dealt them.

Meanwhile, I have DVDs of Moscow and St Petersburg and CDs of Russian Orthodox Church music to enjoy.

La Gioconda

By Anita Langham

After miles of haughty salons, room after room revealing with a triumphal flourish more Empire, glories, gloomy oil paint, and more ormolu, I'd finally reached the famous shrine. When standing at the back I noticed, lurking in a shadowy corner, straining with that hard smoothness only marble has, with a wicked grin suffusing his little marble features, a little marble kid was busy throttling a marble goose. He looked like my lad, or maybe yours, engrossed, absorbed, utterly determined, both legs braced and sturdy, chubby arms around the snaking neck, his dimpled fingers held on tight, chiselled features shiny with hot effort, his expression one of sheer delight. Excited, humbled in their icon's presence, fired by their costly catalogues, the worshipers zoomed in, pointed cameras, lifted phones on sticks, everyone oblivious to that desperate struggle in the corner, the frozen downbeat of the bird's frantic pinioned wings, of that tell-tale stone-stain beneath its tail, that sudden splash of fear. The lad grinned, hung on in there, and stared empty-eyed past eager, pushy people to where, beautiful, sallow, the flowering of a different age sat serenely, screened by the armoured glass. Then a grin da Vinci never painted began to spread, to crack her eggshell skin as Mona Lisa looked across the room. Straight at me! Lads, eh? We both thought it. We'd have said it too, but the goose was making such a noise. So, we exchanged a certain look, as mothers often do, each catching for one delicious moment, the wry amusement in the other's eyes.

Memories of Anne Gibbons

By Karin Slade

Anne was a keen gardener and a devoted dog owner with a strong preference for rescued collies who were treated almost daily to a six-mile walk.

At one point we both had dogs called Sally which led to some confusion when I took my Sally on a visit to Anne. Both dogs mostly ignored each other but upon arrival, they would disappear into Anne's bedroom for a few minutes before returning to the living room and ignoring each other.

What happened in the bedroom we never did find out.

*****

Haiku
Anita Langham

Donkey Road

Seaside donkey road
rows of bricks help little hooves
struggle for purchase

Trevor's Tin

By David Hamilton

Sitting on his walking frame
Trevor's on the streets again
Thickly wrapped in coat and cap
Yellow tin upon his lap
Fag in hand and badly shaved
Looks much older than his age.

The station arch his favourite space
When he collects for Zoe's place,
Trevor slowly cleans his glasses
As another shopper passes
They would not try to ignore him
If they only knew his story.

He takes the bus six times a week
To collect upon the street
Doesn't call out to the square
Or shake his tin at people there
Just sits quietly half the day
Tin hung on the walking frame
Staring into his warming tea
Stirs a distant memory.
Long ago a tiny mite
Held his finger like a vice
Now he goes six days a week,
Add the years up – twenty-three
Add the money – sixty thousand
Trevor's total keeps on mounting.

Zoe's place is of great use to
Families with uncertain futures
And Trevor found himself a purpose
With the unpaid background workers
Just because a tiny thing
Needed to hold onto him.

Any day in any weather
Chances are that you'll see Trevor
Sitting quietly by the station
Waiting for the next donation,
Those that know him can't reward him
Those that can have twice ignored him
They'll have reasons, what do we know?
But in my eyes, the man's a hero.

Sandman

By Pauline Bennett

He was good with his hands, always had been and this was easy work although bitterly cold in the wind that whistled down the alleyway straight from the sea. But he had been told not to pick a sunny spot. Folk wouldn't feel as sorry for him but equally, the passers-by did seem to feel the cold too and buttoned up their jackets and blew away down the street to the warmth of the shops.

Yesterday he had changed his model with the arrival of another bag of sand and it had been remarkably successful, the 50pences rolling in. All it had taken was the addition of two small puppies, one with its head resting on its paws in front of its mother and the other playfully climbing on its mother's back and looking cheekily up at the shoppers. Yes, he was the seaside town's sandman. An asylum seeker trying to eke out his meagre allowance and this wasn't technically begging, and he wasn't creating any noise. If he was challenged, he simply rolled up the blue plastic sheet on which his models performed, tipped it into his barrow, and walked away.

However, a few days ago, in a more southern and affluent seaside town, his barrow had been stolen. It was a brazen act of theft in broad daylight but he couldn't chase after the lads and leave his sand dogs or the loose change slowly accumulating at his feet. So, it was gone. He did find it later, but the youths had set fire to the tyre and it was now useless. Not to worry, he was young and fit and could shoulder his sand back to the shared house. Not that it was much safer there, camaraderie was not always the order of the day in the house especially since the arrival of the Kurdish lads, three of them and hard as nails. He had learned to keep his distance and stay out of the kitchen when he heard their raucous, filthy laughter.

He wasn't used to this kind of behaviour. These lads were exactly the kind that got refugees a bad name. Thieving and a suspected mugging was their trademark, oh no, better lie low until they left the house or were obviously the worse for drink. So, the sandman carried on, varying his spots and in the spring months it was almost a joy to see the pleasure on people's faces as they admired his handiwork. But it would be so much better to have a proper job and feel that he was contributing to the country he had fled to.

It had been an easy decision to leave Eritrea. His mother had died by the roadside after a beating from rival soldiers and he knew he would be called up soon to the army. So, he left. Many hardships followed, leaving both physical and mental scars but still, he persevered and claimed asylum near a town named Swindon. The various processes had brought him to the Lancashire coastal resort of Morecambe. Not as busy as its pleasure providing neighbour but not a bad place to end up. If times were really bad, he had found a sympathetic café owner who usually had the odd scraps of fish and chips or crusts off the end of loaves of bread and always a cuppa, strange how the English couldn't live without their cuppas!

But in the last few days, the Kurdish yobs had found his sandbag and tipped it all over his bed, and then used it as a toilet. This was no way to live. He had simply given up, walked out of the house, his ears ringing from the jeers, and headed to the beach. The tide was out, so he sat on the sand and, feeling his sand carving tools in his pocket, began a monumental sculpture, a tribute to his mother. It was stupendous, both in size and detail, a sand picture of his mother's last moments on the dusty street of the small African town. When it was completed, he strode determinedly towards the incoming tide, taking no notice of his shoes and trousers soaking in the shallows he walked on. Up to his waist now, but if anyone could have heard him he was singing, a song that had always been on his mother's lips in his younger, happier days. But there was no one to see him or hear him or hold him up to his neck. He turned over and gave himself to the gentle waves and then felt his mother's arms pluck him to a place of joy and peace.

R.I.P. Thomas

Memories of Anne Gibbons

By Pat Atkinson

I remember her laid-back approach to whatever task was set for writing homework, always doubting she would be able to come up with anything to fit the brief. 'This is rubbish,' she would say at the next meeting when it was her turn to read her work to the group. It never was, as the following piece, written by Anne, attests.

*****

Haiku
Anita Langham

Plastic windmills
whirring on sticks
summer's over

An Important Decision

By Anne Gibbons

We have all been making decisions from the time we had to decide whether we would like a red lollipop or a green one. Some are trivial and don't take much to think about; others can be agonising and life-changing. One decision that affects most people sooner or later is troubling me now. When is the right time to give up driving?

I don't like driving very much and I never have done. I only learned to drive because otherwise, it meant three buses to get to work. Why then should it be difficult to make up my mind? Surely the simplest thing to do is to give it up, after all in this area we have easy access to a good train and bus service, and we don't live in the back of beyond. What is the problem? Well, a car is useful for carrying things and helping people. It means I don't have to hang around waiting for buses or trains which may be late or not arrive at all. Although it is easy to get to Darlington and from there to most of the country as long as you want to go North or South. It is not so easy getting to Errington Woods to walk the dog without a dreary walk up the hill to start with. It isn't easy to get to garden centres, and it isn't easy to visit my friend in Norton who is seriously disabled and can't get into a car. The journey takes half an hour in the car and at least two hours on the bus. To visit a friend in a care home in Redcar takes about eight minutes in the car and at least twenty minutes in the bus – if it turns up. Nowadays I don't need to travel great distances, can ignore motorways altogether and quite enjoy driving locally. I have driven for nearly forty years without killing anyone, but I don't want to start now.

Well, Anne, perhaps you aren't ready to give up yet, just drive sensibly within your limitations. Why do you think you should give up? For one thing, I am getting older and therefore slower in reaction time. Also, my vision is deteriorating slowly as I have some degree of macular degeneration. The DVLA in its wisdom now requires my licence to be reviewed annually. I do not want to be a risk to myself or anyone else. Should I go before I am pushed? An incident that occurred a few weeks ago made me think that the time had come. Going to visit my friend in a care home in Redcar, I don't park in their miserable little car park but in a big public car park in Roseberry Square which usually has plenty of space. To my horror, as I was navigating myself slightly obliquely into a clear space with lots of clear spaces around it, I heard a crunch and a scrape along the side of my car. I had had an altercation with a bollard. After I had spent some time cursing and spitting feathers, I thought to myself this is it. If you can manage to hit a bollard in a pretty empty car park, it is definitely time to give up. Guilt-ridden, I rang the person responsible for the maintenance of the car park and asked if I needed to pay for repainting of the wretched bollard as much of its yellow paint was now adorning the side of my car.

"No, don't worry about it," said the man, "people are doing it all the time."

Now, where am I with this decision-making?

Whether to give up or not to give up is the question.

*****

Haiku
Anita Langham

Confusion

Sea slides, horse looks down
legs cross, confused hooves tangle
in the flattened surf

My Husband's Mistresses
(A Love Story)

By Michael Kirke

As I look back I remember the other females in my husband's life … mine too, for we were all intertwined in our different ways.

Where the last one came from nobody knew, except that she had been in the slammer for nine months. With elegant legs that went on forever and the sauciest walk, she attracted men all right. What's more, she made up to them shamelessly. Despite this, I could not help liking her, for at heart, she was a really nice girl called Saffron. A lovely bewitching name that suited her gentle nature.

In some ways, I was quite happy to be the grass widow when she went off hunting with him. I tried it once or twice with the one before but it's such a dead bore I can't see why Mr Blair makes all that fuss. Anyhow off they went, leaving me alone while they ran around following beagles through mud and rain, not my idea of a turn-on! *He had tried it on with the first one but she had no more liking for cold moorlands than I.* Sometimes he kept her out for a Hunt Tea and Sing but more often he would bring her back for a bath and a meal. Well, how would you feel … but you see, I'd come to love them both, warts and all. You may ask why I put up with the situation, but I just took pity on these two muddy souls. How many of us wives have grown-up little boys in our lives who ask nothing more than to play in the wet and mud?

We had nine months of it. Oh yes, she shared our home, you know, except she had rooms of her own. Apart from that she was in on everything my husband and I did together. Our little trips to the seaside and other outings were always made *a trois*. How would you cope? *The other one had even been on business trips with us before we retired and shared holidays too.* She also had the trick of making strangers relaxed in her presence. Maybe that's why we all got on so well.

You get used to it quite quickly when they put themselves out to please. It's amazing, isn't it how a charming female can make herself greatly liked by both sexes?

In the end, it was all over quite suddenly leaving us both bereft. Can you believe I even accompanied him to the hospital to bid her goodbye? She looked so beautiful as she died quietly in his arms while I held her hand. Oh, my God! We comforted each other all the way home and stopped at an antique centre where we bought some sweet little liqueur glasses in her memory. I told you she was a charmer, and she gave so much in return for our hospitality.

My situation reminds me of the book 'The Grey Mistress' in which a naval wife describes her husband's ship as his first love. But then it's the last love that counts, isn't it?

Other women's men may be besotted by model trains, ball games, stamps, or other such incomprehensible activities. Mine always falls for these graceful leggy Lurcher bitches with limpid eyes and beautiful colouring. And although I love them too, we'll have a terrier next.

A Modern Cinderella

By Molly Griffin

Now Cindy was a single mum
A girl of the Eastenders type,
She could be loud and brash a bit
Then sisters would lard a swipe.

No longer free to enjoy her nights
And well harassed up to here,
Thinking of her past schoolmates
Carousing with pints of beer.

With one hand on her mobile phone
Her toddler, Tom, out of sight,
Cindy's mam won't help at all
She meanly ignores her plight.

Her sisters they are just the same
They think they're cool and glam,
With hair all dyed, tattoos all placed
And bodies wise as a tram.

Cindy's tired of being used
And Tom keeps gnawing at her phone,
She sighs again and feels right down
Wanting some time on her own.

Through the door, the two beauties burst
Kicking Tom's bricks away,
"Here our Cind, borrow us yer shoes
I ain't got cash 'till Friday's pay."

Sister two throws tee shirts in
"You've lots of time just wash these through,
I need one on tomorrow night
And yer net tights – I'll lend 'em too!"

"See, our Cind, we've dates at club
You can't go because of 'im,
We're looking slimmer can you see?
And there's blokes out there we met at t'gym!"

Out they bounced with heads in the air
While Cindy kicks the door 'till it shuts,
I wish those two would just get lost
And I wish lots more for those two sluts!

Then who should come but her neighbour dear
Who's heard the rumpus and comes to see,
She picks up Tom and soothes him down
"We'll sort it all with cups of tea."

And later, Cindy dressed up to kill
Out on the town, with chips for meals.
The neighbour's at home so all is safe,
So she totters along on stilt-like heels.

Alas, the pavement's not made for glam
She runs and her heel sticks in a crack,
But lo and behold a young man appears
And without any fuss, he just has the knack.

He holds up the shoe with heel broken off
But they gaze at each other and break into laughter,
For what was a bad day and seemed to be tragic
Is now what we all know as
HAPPY EVER AFTER!

Primroses for Don

By Pat Atkinson

The primroses were blooming in the wood; a sure sign that spring has arrived at last. Don had hoped to see this floral carpet once more. However, he passed away peacefully one month ago after a long illness that had accelerated rapidly as the New Year came in.

Always upbeat, he hoped to walk in his favourite Rifts Wood once more. I knew this was not likely to happen and I truly believe he did too, but he did not want to let me down.

We knew one another as teenagers through various youth activities and although nothing developed then, we were re-acquainted at a mutual friend's wedding, and by our thirties we were married. Children followed, and Saltburn became our home once more.

"Come on, Bruno, let's do this. Come on, boy." As I attached the leash to Bruno's collar his mournful eyes expressed more than words could say.

We were soon descending the narrow pathway of pounded earth towards First Fairy Glen. The familiar sound of the trickling stream and the sensuous aroma of the woodland suffused my body, and I drew in a refreshing and calming breath. I could hear voices. My family was waiting.

Marty, our grandson, read a poem, and our granddaughter Hayley said a prayer.

A Song of Spring by Mary Howitt

See the yellow catkins cover
All the slender willows over;
And on mossy banks so green
Star-like primroses are seen;
And their clustering leaves below
White and purple violets grow.

Hark! The little lambs are bleating,
And the cawing rooks are meeting

In the elms ... a noisy crowd;
And all birds are singing loud.
There, the first white butterfly
In the sun goes flitting by.
Thank you, God, for the birds and flowers
Thank you, God, for all the hours
Spent in joyous reverie

In this lovely special place.
Fill us with your grace that we
Will always treasure the times we spent
Running, jumping, climbing chasing
Building dens, exploring nature
Grandad, you will always be in our hearts
God Bless. Amen

We scattered Don's ashes in silence. "It was a fitting final act for Dad," Julie, our daughter, said.

"It was fitting, love, but not final as Dad will always be here in spirit in this most beautiful setting."

Bruno barked unexpectedly, prompting us to turn sharply towards him, and at that moment I truly believed our faithful Labrador sensed the importance of the moment. Any tension we had felt during our little ceremony eased. Bruno had diverted our melancholy.

Lost in my thoughts I re-ran a line from the poem,
and on a mossy bank so green
Star-like primroses are seen ...
(Mary Howitt Writer and Poet, 1799-1888)

Our task completed we began to climb the path out of the glen. Life will go on. God Bless. Amen.

Memories of Anne Gibbons

By Rita Beckham

Anne was such a lovely lady. She loved her dog taking her for walks each day!
She wrote every day. Be it her diary, her memoirs, or short stories.
She liked to read extracts from her memoirs to me and she had a beautiful reading voice.

*****

Haiku
Anita Langham

Wind blows flaxen manes
of reeds, sun in water slips
through countless stems

Twilight Memories

By Molly Griffin

In the in-between light, we were wild,
Young and giddy at the hour forgotten.
The sun blazed daily, but now almost testing,
Approaching glimmer brought mystery and magic.

We had turned the half-green grass for days
With wooden rakes that scratched and gathered
stalks,
We children shared and worked hardest – we said,
Disturbing skittering mice, strewing, fading
flowers.

That precious drying grass, I see still with its
summer scent.
We slurped water and cold tea bottled, dripping
stream cooled.
Our powerful, gentle horses stood shaking their
heads,
Never impatient, but whisking evening tickling
things.

The hay cart was laden as the men forked and heaped
fast,
There was a thundery feeling in the air – they said.
Joy on joy we climbed and almost thrown a-top,
And our well-loved horses steadily lumbered up
the lane.

High hedges hide little rustlings and squeaks,
The last light lingered and the glow from lamps
hovered,
We hushed ourselves, perhaps forgotten in the
shadows,
Hopeful for more time in that other world
Where the half-light secretly darkened and we

were free,
The warmth crept around us still on our last ride.
Sharply, the calls came, as we knew they would
And we were loathed to leave and be chivvied,

So hay scratched and scuffed we gave up,
surrendered.
But the tight-packed barn with its warm grassy
smell,
Would beckon us again to gather laughing and
daring.
Years later, those magical twilights are
remembered,
Another life, of enchanting, busy days in
hedge-rimmed fields.

White Island

By Roger Elgood

Black Jake was misnamed. He was an albino. From the crown of his head where the hair grew in long snowy locks to the soles of his enormous feet whereon, if one ignored their un-washed state, no natural pigment could be perceived, and his body was free of all colouring. His eyes, as is usual in albinos, were pink, indicating that his blood, at least, was of normal consistency, but all cuts, scars, and blemishes, of which there were many on his repellent body, remained unpleasantly fishy white.

Why then, the name? Perhaps it came from the black patch worn in true piratical fashion over his right (starboard) eye, but it is more likely that it referred to his heart or wherever such emotions as he possessed resided. He was a man without pity. Black Jake was feared throughout the oceans by all mariners. All but one. That one now surveyed Black Jake as he struggled and cursed in a futile attempt to break free of the ropes and chains which bound him.

The battle between the two pirates, Harry (Hooker) Hodgson and Black Jake had lasted for three hours and only come to an abrupt conclusion when an unnecessary but still burning cigar butt had dropped, unnoticed, through an open crack in the deck onto an emergency store of gunpowder. The resultant explosion had rendered Black Jake's schooner, The Immodest Mermaid, unserviceable for anything other than firewood and had transformed most of her crew prematurely and instantly into highly nutritious fish food. The remainder of Black Jake's crew had quickly followed their unfortunate shipmates on their journey to Davy Jones's locker, leaving Hooker Hodgson with the interesting problem of what to do with his adversary. Hooker had reluctantly admitted to himself that 'further persuasion' employing his unorthodox but messy methods of inducing loquacity were unlikely to produce any useful information. No maps, with 'X marks the spot' had been found on the prisoner's person, and all that Jake had offered in response to Hooker's enthusiastic questioning had shocked the victor's insensitive soul with their profanity.

So, what to do with Black Jake, a man without whom the world would surely be a better place?

With such chivalry as Hooker retained, he felt it would not be fitting just to slit Jake's throat and tip him over the side. Easy, but lacking in finesse. Then the idea occurred to him.

"We'll take him to White Island," he told Mopey Dick, his lugubrious lieutenant, "and there we'll line him up against the cliff and have a shooting match. It might scare him into telling us where all his loot is stashed, and if it doesn't, well, target practice never did anyone any harm."

White Island wasn't an easy place to find. It had lain undiscovered for centuries and even when found, had been considered such a dismal place as hardly worth marking on the charts. Seabirds and guano and nothing else. Hooker was interrupted in his musings by a shout from the masthead, "Land ho! Two points on the starboard bow." Much relieved because navigation was still, for him, more a matter of fortune than finesse, Hooker confirmed that it was, indeed, White Island and, as they drew nearer, issued instructions for Black Jake to be placed in the long boat for his final journey to land. The remainder of the crew would come ashore in whatever boats were available. The craft containing the two pirate captains, one victor and the other vanquished, touched the beach with a soft, evil-smelling slurping sound. There must have been rock somewhere below the surface, but all that was visible were acres of guano and acres of birds. One cannot have guano without birds and White Island owed almost its entire existence to millions of sea birds of all shapes, sizes, and ages. The indigenous inhabitants took little initial notice of the intruders as they disembarked. Indeed, the only incident of note was when Hooker, glancing upwards and momentarily forgetting the prosthesis which gave him his name, went to wipe away an importunate offering from a passing seagull and was only saved from requiring a black patch by the quick thinking of the Bosun, who grabbed his arm.

Black Jake was hustled forward and positioned under a convenient overhang of the cliff. Hooker's crewmen then proceeded to prepare their motley assortment of firearms. Black Jake, while defiant, was understandably nervous. Facing death from an impromptu firing squad can unsettle the most bloodthirsty of pirates. He viewed the preparations uneasily. When all was in order, Hooker Hodgson readied himself to give the signal for the first volley. Black Jake's nerve broke.

"Stop!" he screamed, "I'll tell you where it's all buried."

The sound of his voice echoed from cliff face to cliff face. Suddenly the air was full of birds, startled by the unnatural sound of the human shout. Countless millions of them soared into the sky, jostling for air space and all startled by this unexpected disturbance. The next second, all that could be heard was the sound of thousands of tons of guano falling in individual pellets, evacuated from the cloacae of countless millions of assorted avian lives. This disgusting discharge, this faecal fusillade, descended from above in a never-ending, ever-increasing avalanche of evacuation. Within seconds, Captain Hodgson and his crew were stuck to the ground. Within moments they were imprisoned to their knees, then their thighs. By the time the downpour of droppings had ceased, the sticky mess was up to their waists. And then the sun came out, shining on White Island with more than tropical splendour, and everyone, with the sole exception of Black Jake, was imprisoned in a stinking, rock-hard mass of guano that had set with a strength greater even than Portland cement. But Black Jake was bound in ropes and while he was spared the worst of this deluge of dung, escape was as impossible for him as for his captors.

Sometime in the future, when the need for guano as a fertiliser has risen sufficiently to justify the expense of mining, the bodies of these marine malefactors may be found. One wonders what the discoverers will make of it all.

Ladybird, Ladybird

By Anita Langham

"FIRE! FIRE!" Ladybird screams.

"Oh yes?" murmurs a Lacewing performing graceful aerobatics over the pond. "Sounds like fake news to me."

"No, it's right – me house is on fire! Me kids are all gone! Have you seen 'em?"

Her lovely wings barely miss a beat as Lacewing banks sharply and circles Ladybird's reed. "How many are involved, exactly?" she enquires languidly.

"Um, our Ann crept under the fryin' pan, so that's twelve still missing."

"What do they look like, exactly?"

"Like... sort of sawn-off black caterpillars."

"Good grief! I can't imagine what your husband must be like..."

"That swine tittled off and left me with the lot, hasn't he? Oh, and they're covered in spikes and knobbles if that helps at all."

"How awful for you!" cries the Lacewing, shooting up vertically and flicking all six legs in a horrified entrechat. "Are you sure you want them back?"

"Oh yes, and did I mention the orangey bits?"

"Nooo, but that narrows it down – I think I'd remember such ghastly creatures. Now if you wouldn't mind, I'm rather busy with my aerial display – we *Chrysopae* are internationally renowned for it, you know."

And Lacewing resumes her spectacular dance: figures of eight, wing-waggles, looping-the-loop – all the time admiring her reflection in the water from every angle.

"Have *you* seen my kids, mister?" Ladybird shouts down to a Sexton Beetle beavering away on the bank. "This magpie dropped a burning fag-end on our high-rise bug hotel, see? It only had the wrong sort o' cladding, didn't it? Went up like the towerin' inferno!"

"Oh aye?" The Sexton, who's busy burying a dead shrew, pauses and casts a beady eye over the speaker. "What sort of a mother do *you* call yourself? Why were they home alone anyway? You held regular fire drills, I hope? Had you installed smoke alarms? Sprinklers? Fire doors? How many fire extinguishers did you have? Serviced annually, were they?"

"You must be jokin'– I can't afford all that pizzaz! I was maxed out on me credit cards and me Universal Credit still hasn't come through – I'm strugglin' just to put aphids on the table."

"Typical..." says the Sexton, going back to his digging. "Poorly educated, too many children... bone idle, living off benefits, spending money willy-nilly that isn't yours to spend. Holidays with expensive flights, no doubt. Drink and drugs too, I shouldn't wonder... Oh no," he says, twitching his antennae in disapproval. "Don't expect any sympathy from me."

Ladybird feels herself losing it. "I don't want ruddy sympathy, I want me kids! Have you seen 'em or not? Oi! Where've you gone, you miserable old beggar?"

The Sexton has disappeared under the dead shrew, so his voice is muffled. "We *Nicophori*," he huffs, "are responsible – citizens, unlike some! We do important – work," he puffs, "for the good of society and the – planet, in fact–"

He is interrupted by a thin, high-pitched wail because, intent on her reflection, Lacewing has clipped a reed and ploughed into the water like a seaplane doing a belly-flop. Her gossamer wings flutter like lace curtains through an open window, then, swamped and sodden, they sink below the surface. Her slender body follows, her struggles become more and more feeble – and she drowns.

"Women drivers," mutters the Sexton, who has beetled out from under the shrew and is excavating the other side. Soil flies in all directions as he digs deeper and deeper. "Should never've been allowed in the air," he grumbles, stepping back to admire his legwork.

Ladybird's about to give him a mouthparts-full when the reed she's balancing on begins to wobble and sway. Squinting down its length, she sees an Emperor Dragonfly struggling to exuviate himself from his larval case.

"At last…" says the dragonfly. He arches his turquoise body and, with one final effort, wriggles free. Keeping a tight hold of the reed, he stretches luxuriously. "That's better – it was rather cramped in there." He vibrates his damp, crumpled wings to pump some blue blood around the veins. As they dry and expand, the sunlight streams through them and casts rainbows across the water. Suddenly, the mirror-like surface is shattered as the Sexton takes a step too far backwards, falls head over thorax over abdomen, into the pool! SPLISH! SPLASH! SPLOSH!

Ladybird watches the beetle spinning around on his back like a crazy coracle. Oh dear, she thinks. Ignore the Health & Safety notices, did we? But she's a kindly soul, so of course, she doesn't say it.

The Emperor has no such compunction. He watches scornfully as Sexton's struggles grow weaker and weaker till they cease. "Peace comes to the pool," he sneers. "This area is so going downhill."

"Show a bit of respect," Ladybird protests.

"Oh, forgive me, Your Eminence," says the Emperor, trying to focus all his eyes on the red-rimmed undercarriage teetering above him. "I didn't notice you up there on your throne!"

Ladybird is overwhelmed to find herself in such close proximity to royalty but feels obliged to put a word in for the Sexton. "Pardon me if I'm speaking out of turn," she ventures, "but at least he was doing his bit for the environment by recycling. What have you ever done?"

"I," says the Emperor haughtily, "don't have to do anything at all." His beautiful wings are almost ready to take flight now, almost ready to convey him to his rightful place in the scheme of things. As he exercises them he feels the power surge through every segment of his jewel-bright body. "And now my eyes are all working together, I see you're not a Cardinal Beetle after all! You're nothing but a– common *coccinella*!"

"Beg pardon, Your Majesty," Ladybird says in her poshest voice, "but I hev mislaid meh offspring!"

"Oh, hard luck," says the Emperor. "Your nanny should be severely reprimanded."

"She shall be given a right bollicking, Sire. In the meanwhile, may one impose upon your Highness to keep all your eyes open for—"

"Know your place! You can't bother an *Odonata* with your plebian concerns – you're banished from this pond! Go back to your deprived area and crawl under a leaf or whatever it is you—" but before he can complete his decree, a sand martin hunting midges over the water, distracted by this rich sparkle of diamonds, rubies, and sapphires, swerves and snatches him on the wing! Darting away across the pool, she dives down her burrow in the sandy bank. From somewhere deep inside, the peeping of her young rises to a crescendo, then all is still.

"I may as well fly away home, I suppose," Ladybird sighs. Casting one last look at the submerged bodies of Sexton and Lacewing, she raises her wing cases and is about to unfold her wings for lift-off when, beyond the dead shrew, she detects a movement. As her eyes focus, a blur of orange and black resolves itself into a collection of spikes and knobbles on legs – then, led by Ann, all thirteen lost children come trooping into view.

"WHAT'S FOR TEA, MAM?" they chorus.

"Little monsters," says Ladybird fondly, "I've been worried sick about you. Hope you like burnt aphids…"

Chalk Dust

By Sarah Telfer

~ The Cliffs of Dover are crumbling into the sea. ~

Forty-thousand years BC
Microscopic plankton like me
Died in our trillions we
Fell into bed with
Our skeletons pressed
Together at one with rock.

We dead-legged waves,
Saw blue birds over
Our white cliffs of Dover.
Us giants of plankton we still
Tower the English Channel,
Too soon we will crumble in salt winds,

Yet here we will make our stand,
Raked by the tide
Daubed in ancient caves
Spilled on the lines of a tennis court –
You cannot be serious?

We are polishing pool cues
Or teeth, or guiding a tailor's hands as
She marks up suits for a wedding.
Look how we powder rough palms

As you mop your brow of me
I will help you lift that weight.
To sir with love we want
To know what YOU will do before
A board rubber crushes our world,
 Back to chalk dust.

Memories of Anne Gibbons

By Marie Arthur

One day, Anne had a dental appointment. The young, good-looking dentist asked if she was going out with anyone after. Thinking, 'Is he going to ask me out?' she replied guardedly, "No one in particular."
However, his reply was rather deflating.
"Because your jumper is inside out."

*****

Haiku
Anita Langham

Torch scatters shadows:
horns, startled eyes on wet walls,
aurochs drawn in blood

The Waiting Game

By Norma Cuthbert

Let me paint a scene for you, a scene of confusion. I was surprised at this cacophony of noise in this sacred space. Never in all my years of attendance had this ever happened.

I arrived ten minutes before my doctor's appointment, not expecting to be delayed, so you can imagine how my heart sank at this sight. Confronting the receptionist for an explanation, she shrugged her shoulders and smiled. I found a chair and viewed all my adversaries. They all became my enemies.

Sat in a corner, I noticed a young mother nursing a child of about two years old. As she read from a storybook, she constantly soothed and caressed her child. Maybe she was soothing her worries, doing her best not to portray her anguish. I wished them well.

An elderly lady sat opposite me. She smiled at me in acknowledgement. Shuffling to make myself more comfortable, I noticed that one of her legs was completely bandaged. 'Ha, bless!' I thought she had had a fall. Had she ulcerated skin under that bandage? I guess I will never know, for she slipped into dozing as her walking stick fell to the floor.

I closed my eyes and asked for patience. The buzzer went for the next one in. More people arrive. Amongst them was a young man, ashen face obviously in shock. His arm was wrapped in a towel and I could see blood seeping through. He seemed unsure about where he was. Thankfully, he was not alone. Bless him. Wait till his mum finds out! He skips the waiting queue.

Ha me, never mind, there is always someone worse off.

A scene catches my eye. Trying not to stare, trying not to intrude, an elderly lady holds and comforts a young girl. She sits with her arm around her, occasionally whispering as she gently strokes her hand, the young girl is tearful. Hope all will be well.

With the gentleman sitting beside me I sympathise. He is agitated, oh how he does try to settle to read his newspaper, constantly looking at his watch, rustling the paper, and shuffling in his seat. Guess by now he needs to be somewhere else.

My time was not wasted. I sat there observing my fellow men. None of us want to be here, but fate's hand seems fit to stop by and pay us a visit. As a result, we have to stop and submit. Lessons to be learned, regrets overcome. May we never stop learning.

A Welcome Sound

By Molly Griffin

Such an awkward month is March, workload full,
Plagued with skittering, fitful winds, gentle then
raging.
With icy rain battering and overfilling ditches.
Streams steal new ways, breaking banks to please
themselves.
The sheep have long since been sheltered in
comforting barns,
They are lumbered, dog driven, heavy with unborn
lambs.
Now, they wait, secured and unfussed and all
inside is still.
With scents of flower-filled hay masked with
heavy fleece odour,
The clever farm cat, hidden and warm, spies, and
is alert.
While the farmer quietly checks, watches, and
waits unsettled,
At times, he is at the half-open door, listening.
Some sheep move heavily, awkwardly, eyes staring,
help comes,
And then, echoes the weak bleating of unsteady
lambs.
Suddenly there come shouts and the farmer is
outside
From the open window of the cottage comes a
welcome sound
As the thin, reedy cry of a newborn baby rends the
air.
"Our child!" he shouts, full of joy and the sound
carries inside
To the sheep-cuddled lambs, the cat now sidles
out to watch.
That the new births have signalled spring and
welcomed the future.

Memories of Anne Gibbons

By Karin Slade

Anne appreciated good food, and while known for her red pepper soup, bacon sandwiches, and sticky toffee pudding, she was otherwise a reluctant cook.

Cheese sandwiches and cheese scones were high on her list of favourites, along with magnum ice creams, cream cakes, and the advent of microwave chips were a joy to her.

*****

Haiku
Anita Langham

We drift apart as
cattle do when grass grows sparse
and fresh fields beckon

Invitation to Mr and Mrs Bennett for Christmas Day Lunch (Pride and Prejudice)

By Pauline Bennett

"Oh, Mr Bennett, what have you brought me to? In such a conveyance too! My head is fairly whirling from the speed, I will never recover!"

"My dear, you will be fine. It is a car. Everyone has one or even two, and very convenient it seems too, especially as we would not have arrived in time for tea if we had been in a carriage. Now compose yourself, my dear, and let us go and meet our hosts! You don't have to take everything you see at face value, I am sure."

"But Mr Bennett, where is the parkland? Look, the house next door is so close. Oh! I am overcome!"

The Bennetts were assisted from the car by the young Jacob, their host's grandson, and approaching the house, Mrs Bennett was consoled by the beautiful Ring of Welcome hanging on the porch door, full of holly, ivy, pine cones, and ribbons, something she was familiar with at least.

Opening the door, a charming middle-aged lady, whipping her pinny off declared, "Come in, come in. You are most welcome to the Bennett abode!"

Mr Bennett began to apologise about their late arrival but was cut short by the lady of the house. "Better late than never. Now do come in and let me take your coat, er your cloak. We will have aperitifs in the lounge. Come through."

Mrs Bennett was about to have one of her fainting fits when she saw it in full glory and could only stand amazed and completely in awe.

"Hello, can I call you Grandmama Bennett?" a small girl lisped at her, "Do you like our Christmas tree? We only finished decorating it last night. It has all my grandma's old baubles on, and we bought the new ones with the lights inside. I think it is beautiful."

"Yes, the best of both worlds," smiled her mother. "But let Mr and Mrs Bennett sit down at least."

Safely settled on the soft luxurious sofa, Mrs Bennett began to relax and take in her surroundings. The tree was indeed magnificent and a vague memory came to her of a picture in a lady's periodical of Queen Charlotte with such a tree in Windsor Castle.

There was a fire crackling in the hearth and the mantlepiece was festooned with greenery and candles and in the centre of the wide doorway leading to the dining room was a sprig of mistletoe. Turning to Mr Bennett, she admitted that even Jane would approve.

Lunch was served and once seated at the groaning table, Mrs Bennett was relieved to see that she recognised certain foods. No goose in the centre of the table but a large, deliciously scented leg of pork surrounded by a variety of sweetmeats and vegetables. "This is my grandma's traditional honey roast pork, she makes it every year and it is marinated for two days before cooking. You'll love it and the pigs in blankets and stuffing," explained the lispy little girl. Before they could be served, long, glittery tubes were being passed around amidst a banging and squeals of delight as the Christmas crackers were pulled. Mr Bennett was in his element, pulling crackers and even cajoled his wife into trying one, and was delighted by her response to the small gift of a silver charm in the shape of an E.

"Oh, Mr Bennett, Lizzie must have this!" she said, although drew the line at the paper hat as it would never fit over her bonnet.

The meal reached a climax with the arrival of a flaming plum pudding which she recognised but was immediately nonplussed when her hostess announced that anyone who didn't want a piece could have Yule Log instead. Seeing the look of horror pass over her face, young Jacob explained, "It's made of chocolate. I believe you used to burn Yule logs but we have a gas fire so that's not possible."

Lunch finished, the party returned to the lounge where all sorts of party games commenced. Mrs Bennett remained firmly in her chair by the strange gas fire that never seemed to be replenished and did concede that Kitty and Lydia would have loved this!

After a little nap, cups of tea were brought in and a piece of a magnificently decorated Christmas cake was given out. Mr Bennett was in heaven, or so he thought to himself. A little while later, a ringing sound emanated from young Jacob's pocket.

"Oh, it's your taxi. It's waiting outside," he announced, and before they realised, they were once more being whisked along prettily decorated streets to their lodgings in the nearby town.

"Well," Mr Bennett said, "you enjoyed that, my dear. As I said before, never take things at face value! Happy Christmas, Mrs Bennett!"

Woman in the Shop

By Molly Griffin

The woman in the shop stands
Stands and breathes in the soft breaths of flowers
Gently smiling she is looking but not seeing
And feels the fall of delicate petal showers
She feels also the smooth satin dress she wore,
Sees the laughing group and knows her side
The man she loves and his gentle holding hand
Then – the woman in the shop, no longer a bride
Moves through the mingling of scents to stay,
Pausing beside a rose of velvety creamy pink.

For she remembers the gift – the key of the door
Something special a marking of years
And smiles, at those words, now old and
forgotten,
The family bouquet of those roses, creamy pink.

A gift full of love and care, for that milestone.
She moves among the flower-filled vases
Showing the ordinary, the meek and the superior.
Then her mind sees her gardens over the years,
Never tidy, never row planted in her father's way
But growing in mixed jumbles choosing their
place.

So now, the choice is made and she is content.
And she takes two rose stems, wrapped in tissue
Two of the delicate roses of creamy pink
And leaves this place of memories, holding her
prize.

24th April 1942

By David Murray

Flight Sergeant Bill Thompson lay back on his bed. It was almost dawn.

It had been a terrible night. The flak over Dusseldorf had been heavier than usual and there seemed to be more 109s than ever. The squadron was already short of planes and had seen at least one of their Lancasters go down in a ball of flames. That left ten of the original fifteen assuming that was the only one, but he had a feeling that it wasn't. Thank goodness there were no ops scheduled for the coming night.

He'd barely settled down Into a re"tles', fitful sleep when a hand shook him roughly by the shoulder. Thompson checked his watch – 16.00 hours. It was the Duty Officer.

"On your feet, Sergeant. Briefing at 18.00 hours number 6 Hangar."

Tempted as he was to simply turn over and go back to sleep, he realised he could not.

"I bet the poor bastards'll be over Dusseldorf again tonight."

At least it wasn't far to go. Despite himself, he made his way to number 6 Hangar, where, to no surprise, several members of his crew were already standing. He recognised his Rear Gunner, a Welshman, David Jones.

"We're off again tonight, Skipper. It's Dusseldorf."

Thompson was only slightly surprised. The Brass did what they wanted. It was only when they were over The Channel and testing their weapons that the reaction set in. He was still dog-tired from the previous night, and the fact that they'd actually lost two Lancasters finally sunk in. He may have been informed, but if he had, then nothing had registered.

Shortly afterwards, they were joined by another two squadrons and it became obvious that they were not far from their target. Thompson's Kite shuddered violently as flak peppered the sky around them. He could feel the heavy shrapnel slicing through the fabric of the Lancaster and tried desperately to ignore it. He failed. Then the Rear Gunner yelled, "There's a 109 coming up fast behind us. Take evasive action."

Actively locked into his bombing run, Thompson couldn't react. There was a loud bang and the entire plane shuddered violently.

"You okay, Taff?" The Flight Sergeant spoke, "Yeah, Skipper, he's banked away." Another voice broke in. "We've lost the whole tail, Skipper. Taff's bought it." It was the Upper Gunner.

"How the hell could we? We're still flying. Anyway, I've just been talking to him."

There was a muttered reply that the pilot couldn't make out when Thompson became aware of the intense pain in his left leg. He reached down and his hand came away covered in blood. He glanced across at the Flight Engineer, who simply sat staring straight ahead as though nothing had happened.

Pilot to Navigator, "Where the hell are we, Charlie?"

"Should be crossing the English Coast anytime now. See the Humber soon."

Relieved but still highly confused, Thompson glanced out to his left. He couldn't see a thing. It was then that he realised that although all four engines were running, they weren't making a sound. He looked up through the canopy and still couldn't see anything. No stars, no moon, no nothing – only what seemed to be a thick violet haze. He reached down to touch the gaping wound on his leg but couldn't feel anything – not even the leg itself.

Amazingly the plane was climbing at a very steep angle. He tried to counteract it and failed. It was as though the machine was flying itself. They were already far higher than it was designed for. He tried one more time to level out and failed then slumped back into his seat.

His last conscious thought was for the rest of the crew. What had happened to them? What had happened to him?

Then, finally, he no longer cared.

Memories of Anne Gibbons

By Barbara Spight

Anne was an early member of Saltburn District u3a and over the years was a member of a wide variety of groups. Anne was a keen writer within the creative writing group and found great pleasure and solace with the singing group.

Anne was also a member of the u3a Reading Group and, occasionally of the Theatre Group. I remember she loved dogs and often wrote about them.

She also told me that she would have loved to come with the Theatre Group to whatever show I was putting on but didn't want to leave her dog home alone.

In the Reading Group, we all used to laugh because she used to tell us that she always turned to the back to see how the story ended.

*****

Haiku
Anita Langham

Cold gold stare on
blue water forget-me-not
an emerald frog

U3a and Me

By Pauline Tweddle

I've learned to play bowls through the u3a
I know how to score for home and away
There's more to this game than you may think
The grass we play on is called a rink.
The bowls are called woods and we aim for the jack,
But sometimes it's easier to give others a smack.
If your wood touches the jack it's called a kiss,
But if it's too heavy you're sure to miss.
"Too narrow" may come the call from the Skip
I try to go wider and land in the dip
I don't rant and rave it's not etiquette
Or whoop and shout or pirouette
I just shake hands with the opposing team
Good game I say with a touch of yearning
Forgive me for the errors as I'm just learning.

I used to Tap Dance at Coatham Hall
We'd warm up first from wall to wall
A hop and a shuffle and a cha-cha through
With maybe a chassis and a ball spring too
Moving arms and a kickball change
With time steps and wings as part of our range.
Country dancing I do with Paul
Not too difficult if you listen to his call
We join together in a star
Then a circle but not too far
A right and left through and a doe cee doe
Followed by a chassis but not too slow
We hoot and laugh when we get it wrong
And even sometimes join in the song
Thursday afternoon is such a treat
We even get tea and biscuits to eat

ANNE'STHOLOGY

Once a month on Friday at ten
I help Geoff decide what to play when
We listen to music from every ilk
From Mozart to Motown and Acker Bilk
It's good to listen and just sit still
It does more good than taking a pill

There's lots of activities in the u3a
Quite a lot to fill your day
There's walking and talking and singing for
pleasure
Many pastimes to fill your leisure
You can learn to speak Russian, Italian, or French
Or learn about history and life in a trench
We visit the theatre or maybe a trip
We learn about flora, fauna, and fungi too
With lectures from experts who like what we do
But most of all it's the people we meet
Who now smile and wave when we walk down the
street.

Memories of Anne Gibbons

By Karin Slade

Outside of u3a groups, Anne was a member of the Town's Women's Guild, learned to swim in her sixties, and was a regular member of the congregation at St Bede's church in Marske.

Before Anne's vision deteriorated, she loved to knit, never garments but rather all of the many Jean Greenhow figures that she gifted to the children and grandchildren of her friends.

Another favourite pastime was to visit garden centres – tea, cake, and chat, plus the purchase of a new plant or pot made for a perfect day.

*****

Haiku
Anita Langham

Pippit, wet-steel grey,
rummaging through wave-washed rocks,
dogged as my dreams

A Badly Wrapped Parcel

By Pat Atkinson

The hands were cold that held me tight.
I knew not whether he had the right to dump me
down on the ground,
Bereft, deserted, too dangerous to know because
my bow had come unbound.
He had moved on to smarter things, bigger, bolder
plasticised.
I felt the need to criticise, don't leave me here in a
dark forgotten corner I plead,
I only need a little attention, oh! And I forgot to
mention
I was prioritised, and stamped as such, look I've
got the mark.
I should be delivered next day with the lark.
Don't leave me here you foolish man, I should be
riding in your van.
There's people waiting for my arrival, so please
don't think me tri-vial.
I have a place of great importance at the address
of my client.
At the feast, you'll see me taking centre stage on
the celebration table.
Tommy will be all forlorn if there's no cake to
wish upon.
Don't pinch me, poke me, prod me roughly
there's a masterpiece inside this parcel.
Hold me, caress me, take great care that I may
Soon be there when joyfully the children sing

HAPPY BIRTHDAY TOMMY FLYNN!

Memories of Anne Gibbons

By Pauline Caley

I knew Anne through the Creative Writing Group. She was warm, quiet, and gentle, but acutely witty. Her writing, always enjoyable, could be amusing or very moving and always caught one's attention. Her spoof 'round robin' one Christmas brought on the giggles. How she managed to read it with a straight face, I have no idea.

She once wrote of a baby, found in a local wood, so convincingly that one of us worried about her till the next meeting would clear up its fictional origin.

I remember Anne fondly, particularly for her twinkly eyes, her skill, and her understated comments. I am happy and privileged to have known her.

*****

Haiku
Anita Langham

Phosphorescence
sparkles as diver enters
shower of stars

India

By Pauline Tweddle

So far, my visit to India had been very enjoyable, enhanced by a visit to the Taj Mahal and other awe-inspiring sights.

Today my aunt, with whom I was staying, had some business to attend to in Old Delhi. It was a chance to explore the Old Town on my own for a couple of hours. She took me to a reputable rickshaw stand on Chandni Chowk near the Red Fort and paid the hired driver to conduct me around the sights.

I was looking forward to seeing Jama Masjid, India's largest mosque, Lal Mand, Delhi's oldest Jain Temple, Razia Sutana's tomb and the impressive railway station. We set off amid the general noise and hullaballoo, with crowds of people toing and froing in their bright clothes, searching out the markets and going about their business. There were piles of vividly coloured spices outside the shops, and I could smell the fish market among other pungent smells. The rickshaw driver weaved his way amidst the heavy traffic, animals, and children all vying for a place on the road. After a short distance, another man dressed quite smartly, jumped on the rickshaw, gave the driver some rolled-up rupee notes, and took over the driving whilst the original driver faded into the crowd.

My second driver veered off the main thoroughfare and started darting down narrow side streets, which I was sure were not on the route my aunt had agreed.

"Where are we going?" I asked.

He answered in one gruff word, "Emporium!"

"I don't want to go shopping. I just want to see the sights."

No answer. He just continued peddling.

Next, he pulled up outside a scruffy-looking building, ushered me inside, and gestured to the racks of jewellery on display. It was not what I had planned, but I had promised to buy myself a silver necklace as a souvenir, so might as well do it now. I chose one quickly, keen to get back to my sightseeing before it was time to meet up with my aunt.

"You need to come this way to pay for it," my driver gestured as he led me through a door.

Waking up – I surfaced from under the covers of the bed, stretched languorously, and slowly opened my heavy eyes. Why did my head hurt so much, and why was I wearing only underwear? Where were my pyjamas? I leaned up on one elbow and immediately felt queasy. I was aware of a disoriented swimming sensation in my head and an unbelievable throbbing.

"Mum?" I croaked. "Where are you?"

No answer!

I struggled to sit up and realised I didn't recognise any of the items in the room. Where was I? Panic started to set in as I struggled to remember how I had got here and whether, in fact, I did have a mum. Common sense told me I must have, as it was an instant reaction to call out her name – but what was her real name? I couldn't remember. What was my name? That was even scarier as I couldn't remember that either. What am I doing here? How did I get here? My mind was blank.

There was movement outside the door and a woman wearing a sari came in and called out to someone further away, but I didn't understand the language, so I had no idea what she said.

"Good. Awake at last," said an English-speaking man as he barged into the room. "Here, put these clothes on. It's time to go to work. You can have a quick wash over there at the sink but make it quick. I haven't got all day."

I was utterly bewildered but staggered over to the small bathroom he had indicated and proceeded to do as he had asked.

"Where am I?" I asked.

"Don't you remember?" he said, and when I shook my head, he said, "Good. Now let's get to work."

I had no idea where we were going as he ushered me into a big white car but thought all would come back to me when we got to work. What kind of work did I do? I had no idea. I looked around but did not recognise anything and couldn't understand the cacophony of noise all around as we weaved our way through countless people, animals, children, and wagons blaring their horns.

The noise seemed to exacerbate the throbbing in my head. We drew up at a ramshackle kind of warehouse building and he pushed me through the door.

The place was a factory lined with sewing machines, operated by rows of young girls in Indian type dress sewing diligently, sweating profusely. I was sure I did not work here. I was English that much I knew. My driver handed me over to the man in charge and said he would collect me later, despite my protestations.

"Here, this is your machine. Now get to work sewing those seams and do not waste time!"

I was completely bewildered as I sat down and gazed at the piles of cloth on the table next to the machine. Tears pricked my eyes, and I did not know where to start. The girl on the next desk looked at me with her huge brown eyes and in halting English, offered to help. She showed me exactly what I was supposed to do and left me to get on with it. The headache was easing but now the soreness in my hands, as I pushed the cloth through, was distressing me, and my back was aching.

I knew I did not normally do this kind of work and was sure I did not live in India.

All day I wrestled with questions, willing myself to remember but only getting more confused.

The man in the white car came to take me back but would not answer any of my questions. He thrust me into a house, where the lady I first saw gave me some dahl to eat and some fruit.

She seemed kind, but as she didn't speak any English, she couldn't tell me anything and so led me to the room where I had first wakened up. Feeling exhausted, I climbed into bed.

The next time I woke up I felt much better and tried to make sense of what was going on. Although the amnesia was still present, I seemed to remember foggy images.

Eventually, the man returned and informed me that they had contacted people who knew me, and he had demanded a ransom for my release. He had found a copy of my passport in my handbag, and although he knew who I was, he wouldn't tell me. I had no way of knowing if anybody was able or willing to provide money for a ransom.

"In the meantime," he said, "you work to pay for your keep."

The day wore on as I struggled to stitch the garments under the glare of the overhead light, with sweat prickling my back and beading on my forehead. The water they gave me tasted brackish but was very welcome. Savitri, the kind girl next to me, didn't speak much English, only Urdu, I suppose, but shared her food with me. Images were coming and going inside my head. I was trying desperately to recall my name and who I was.

Late in the day, weighed down with fatigue, I heard a commotion in the back of the room. It was the police accompanied by a lady shouting, "Where is she? Where is she? Linda?"

I vaguely recognised the lady, and Linda struck a chord, so I lunged into the aisle where they could see me.

"Help me!" I called at the top of my voice.

Seventeen From Appomattox

By Michael Kirke

A story of Texan cavaliers making their long journey home across the ruins of a ravaged nation, led by a war-weary Captain.

Breakout, Virginia. April 1865
Michael Kirke

The Confederate scouts on the hillside regarded the Union troops below with disbelief. Frequently outnumbered, they had never before encountered such awe-inspiring forces.

Every road and field was covered with men and equipment.

"Jesus Christ on th'mountain!' said one. "I ain't ever seen such a mess of bluebellies."

"Reckon they produce them out of a factory?" wondered the still elegant Corporal Jack.

"Hell no," the Sergeant replied. "Theyun's some mothers' chilluns, same as we'uns."

"They ain't humankind!" was Micah's bitter comment. "They'all's damn Yankees!"

"What'll we do now?' the Corporal asked. "Looks like th'war's come to a daid stop."

"We high tail it back to th'Cap'n an' give him the glad tidings." the Sergeant replied.

"You reckon he'll have us surrender with Gin'ral Lee an'all?" Micah asked.

"Not Cap'n Redford Thompson! He'll light out back fer Texas ... and I'm ridin' with him," opined the Sergeant winding up with, "Ain't nothin' left fer us in this hyah section. Let's go."

The small scouting party turned their backs on the valley around the village of Appomattox Court House. They worked their way into the deep pine woodlands. Here the remnants of Rodger's Texas Mounted Rangers were the forward screen of the 10th Virginia Cavalry.

Like all of Lee's legendary Army of Northern Virginia, every unit was sadly depleted. Gone were the merry cavaliers who had once ridden rings around their inept Unionist opponents.

In their place were ragged, ill-equipped veterans, still young in years but old in time.

But they'd seen the Elephant. How they'd seen the Elephant!

The Sergeant led his patrol into a well-hidden encampment. He dismissed his men knowing that Corporal Jack would oversee the care of the horses by their owners. A task doubly important now that the War for Southern Independence was past its last legs. He saluted the tall, scarred company officer whose skill and luck had kept the two of them alive ever since they crossed the Mississippi four years earlier. The Sergeant recalled their first meeting when his CO was an eager young recruit. '*The boy turned out better'n most.*' he thought.

Captain Redford Thompson wore his authority as easily as he wore his weathered grey uniform.

"Well, Josh," drawled the Captain as his company's remaining junior officer and NCOs loped over to his fire with that easy rolling gait common to seamen and horsemen the world over. "What've you all found out there?"

The Sergeant took a stick and squatted comfortably as he drew a rough map in the sandy soil saying, "This here's the end of th'line, Cap'n. Leastways as far as regular troops are concerned."

The discussion was interrupted before Red could add to it by a messenger from the Colonel asking the Captain to collect his orders for the morning. Those left behind chewed over their fears some more before concluding that Texas needed them as a viable mounted unit more than General Lee would after making their surrender to overwhelming numbers. They were still chewing on 'ramrod rolls' of overcooked moulded rice baked on ramrods held over the embers when Captain Thompson returned.

Red Thompson looked sadly at the men he had led for so long, just half of those who had joined with hopes flying as high as their banners! He was determined to keep his company under arms to protect the families who had refugeed from isolated frontier settlements attacked by Indians.

He finished his summary, "Now, this is what we're going to do."

Memories of Anne Gibbons

By Karin Slade

Anne was the best friend you could have if you were ill; she travelled many miles in her car and later by bus to visit friends in hospitals and care homes.

I do not think she ever lessened the acerbity of her tongue but those friends knew they were dearly loved. I just hope Anne knew how much she was dearly loved.

*****

Haiku
Anita Langham

Jellyfish, yummie
bags of salty water make
turtle cry salt tears

The Flames Are Gone

By Molly Griffin

We often took the road to the Gare.
A rough trail skimmed by mean, tough grass,
Withstanding the persistent salt winds.
And then we pass the ever-present flames
Almost enclosed in their skeleton of iron,
Still, they symbolise the power of steel.
Beyond, the river busies itself
Taking lumbering ships to awaiting cranes.
Suddenly we stop, for our flames are gone
And something is badly, sadly missing,
The tall grasses are the same, but litter mocks.
Perhaps the fishermen's huts will be a haven,
There is always the daily swept lace-edged beach
Bordered by its salt-loving greenery,
Spied over by sweeping, shouting sea birds.
But in our waiting, we see one lone man,
Overalled, lingering, leaning, lost in thought,
Smoking and reflecting over past years
For the white heat and flames symbolised the prize,
And all his generations shout in useless protests.

Spirit Cove

By Sarah Telfer

Waves scalp the sheer cliff face. A battered sign reads:

SWIM ING   PRO IBIT D

Spirit Cove has claimed six lives in three years.
I shudder as the water drives breath from my lungs. My feet lift from the sandbank, and I glide out into deep water. The sea that visits Spirit Cove is freezing whatever the weather. It is wise to prepare your body for the cold by breathing deeply and slowly, to draw oxygen into the blood and thence into every bodily cell.

You must respect the treacherous currents and know the tides. I have been swimming here for fifty-three years. Every month, I take a detour from my usual route home from visiting my granddaughter and nose my car down the steep road to Spirit Cove.

The cove and I have an understanding.

This is our secret meeting place.

I have only to close my eyes and Jake is swimming beside me in the water.

We would hold competitions to see who could swim the farthest and hold their breath the longest underwater. I usually won the prizes. Belgian chocolates, whiskey – supplied through Jake's dubious contacts. Spirit Cove was a neutral ground where we could spend time together before going our separate ways. He back to the Air Force base, and I back to my mother.

I am swimming towards shore when I hear the crude roar of an engine. A slice of light parries the brow of the hill and lunges down the bank. My heart thumps as I tread water with just my head and shoulders visible. I stare wildly as the motorbike speeds down the hill, swerving to avoid my car, its back wheel fudging grass as it comes to a skidding halt.

The rider sits for a moment astride his motorbike, spitting a barrage of profanity. He throttles the engine and waits while it splutters and dies.

Why oh why did I leave my clothes in the car?

I breaststroke further out. I want to avoid making any sound that can be heard above the waves hissing on the shore. I hear the metallic scrape of a boot on concrete as the motorcyclist swings off his bike, try not to think of the pain his boot could inflict. The helmet is coming off. A torrent of hair spills down his back like dried ribbons of seaweed.

It is fear that prompts my memory of a news item in yesterday's local paper.

The man we are looking for is approximately six feet tall, with a medium build with unusually long dark hair.

Treading water fifty yards from the shoreline, I wait to see if he leaves without investigating my car. A lazy riptide nudges me further out, a discreet reminder to swim for the waves. He strides over to the car, stalks it, then opens the car door and dives inside. Darn, it! I left my keys in the ignition and my handbag on the passenger seat. He emerges from the car holding something. It is not my handbag. Then I remember on the back seat I have a special reserved bottle of Jack Daniel's, a present from Tennessee.

He returns to the bike lifting the bottle to his lips. I wince as he takes a mouthful. It does not seem to bother him that the whiskey is more than eighty per cent proof. He scans the area for signs of life, stretching muscles and unfurling his arms into the air. Both jacket and jeans are slack on him as if he has lost weight. There is what looks like yellow fluorescent paint on the back of his jacket.

Jake owned a similar jacket – minus the paint. After the police handed it back to me, I swore I would keep it forever. Was it last summer or the one before when I finally let it go to a charity shop? Why did I do that?

His left ear was pierced several times. One surviving victim identified a distinctive red and black tattoo of a scorpion on his chest…

He passes the end of the bench and strides towards the railings.

Please do not let it be him.

He gulps my fine whiskey – wasted on his palate – and

places the bottle at his feet. One hand on the safety rail, the other hand searches his breast pocket.

Now he lights a cigarette.

What shall I do? He will surely see me move.

He tosses the spent match onto the beach.

Go away - please go away.

Three waves foam on the sand. His face is in shadow and my sight is blurred by the dark. I see only the glow of the cigarette as he inhales. I doubt by the relaxed position of his body that he has spotted anything too out of the ordinary, though surely, he must have noticed my towel.

He turns to lean back on the rail, massaging stiff muscles on his shoulders, leans his head to the left, lion stretches. When he leans his whole body to the right, his hair shifts to reveal the lettering on the back of his jacket. I think it reads:

ANGEL

As I see it, I have two choices. I either die from hypothermia as the riptide drags me out to sea or take my chances with this bike gang member who may be the man responsible for three vicious attacks on locals.

I swim cautiously towards the shore, desperate for an escape plan. A playful current grips my legs and I yelp aloud as I am dragged sideways.

"Who's out there?" he shouts over the rail.

He sees me. He freezes for several seconds, as an animal does when sighting its prey. Then he sheds his jacket, pounds down the beach to the water's edge, and struggles to untie his boots. The current takes me again and I submerge and swim against it at a slight angle towards the shore. Breaking the surface, I see him throw the still-smoking cigarette into the water as he wades in.

"You almost killed me," he growls. "Stupid place to leave your bloody car – in the middle of the road like that."

"Go away!" I cry, choking back seawater.

His tattooed arms thrash the sea like a waterwheel. I have triumphed over the riptide but he is swimming directly into it, possibly because it looks easier. There are no waves there.

"Go back," I warn him, "You'll be dragged out."

He appears not to have heard.

I fill my lungs with air, dive and swim under him, grab his legs, and pull him under the surface with me. Trapped breath scalds my chest. Nevertheless, I manage to drag him almost to the seabed before letting go. I feel Jake close by, encouraging me to keep going. It takes all my strength to swim back to the beach and crawl out of the sea. My fear has exhausted me as much as the violent exertion on my muscles. I glance behind to see him regain his footing in waist-deep water for him. I am unable to do anything now but lay on my back on the beach to recover my breath. He follows, lurching in the sea, water drains in rivulets from his ripped jeans; phlegm extends from his nose and mouth. Close up I can guess he is in his twenties. His chin is hidden with a beard and his skin is grimed with dirt even the sea could not remove.

He traps his hair behind his ears. There are four earrings in his left ear, and with every movement they clink together like ice in a glass. There is a metal ring through one eyebrow. He produces a knife from his back pocket and with a practised flick of his thumb, the blade snaps open. He is still retching as he plants his knees on either side of my hips. I try feebly to cover my nakedness with my hands and at the same time ward off the seawater that drips from his hair and face.

a vicious and unprovoked attack resulting in the elderly victim's death.

Needle fingers prick my scalp. I dread to feel that blade against my skin. The hand holding the knife is unsteady, the fingernails bitten short. I see reflected in those bleak eyes the despair that floods my eyes. If his attacks are unprovoked, what is he capable of now that I've held him underwater?

I don't want to be his next victim. God help me…

He raises the knife and I, mute with terror, close my eyes to what must come.

Nothing.

My eyes jerk open to see him slice up the front of his t-shirt and plunge the knife into the sand at the side of my head. I try to scream but it comes out like a cross between a groan and a whine. There is no hair on his chest, it is covered instead with a vest of tattoos: skulls, spiders, snakes, and a dragon. A red and black striped scorpion protects his breastbone.

People like me are supposed to give people like him a wide berth.

His mouth splits to reveal a graveyard of teeth. I turn away from the force of his foul breath, improved slightly by my expensive whiskey.

"Don't you know swimmin' ain't allowed here," he snarls, covering me with his ripped t-shirt, "especially skinny-dippin'."

My ribs ache as I gasp for breath. I manage to say: "Good job I was here. You could have drowned." Then regain some of my dignity with his soaked t-shirt.

He stands aside to give me space. I stumble to the bench where I left my towel. I catch him glancing over at me as a cat would keep an eye on a wounded bird.

"Go ahead, get dry. I won't look."

He retrieves his jacket, hunkers down on the sand with a battered tin, and sets about the business of hand-rolling cigarettes.

No sooner have I finished drying myself than a boot slams onto the bench. "You want to watch yourself." He fiddles with the laces. "Out here all alone…"

Too right I have to watch out: for creatures like you.

"Want a smoke?" he grunts, offering one of the rather lumpy and pungent-smelling cigarettes he has just rolled.

I shake my head.

"Please yourself," he mutters, trapping the cigarette between his lips.

He makes a grand ceremony out of the whole business. Lighting the cigarette, sucking the smoke into his lungs, blowing it out through pursed lips. Then he slumps back on the bench and the wooden slats groan beneath his weight. When he inhales, I see ribs press through his skin.

"Good stuff. You sure you don't want some?"

"Certainly not," I protest.

"Pity," he says. "Might loosen you up a bit."

Part of my courage returns and I ask him what he is doing here.

"Meetin' someone who needs sortin' out," is the answer he gives.

"You meetin' someone too?" he asks.

"I used to. He died." *Foolish woman, now you are getting into a conversation with this hooligan.* "Drowned in Spirit Cove."

"You tried to save him. Right?"

I nod. "The riptide was too strong." I remember Jake screaming, "Leave me!"

He takes another swig from the bottle.

I point out to him where Jake carved our initials. Using one finger, he absently traces the carving of the heart, enclosing our initials.

"What does the 'D' stand for?" he asks.

"Dorothy."

This man is extremely dangerous. Members of the public should not approach him under any circumstances…

Once more he draws deeply on the cigarette and blinks the smoke out of his eyes.

"As you said, the current was too strong. No point in blaming yourself," he says, picking up the whiskey bottle and taking another drink. "A mate of mine died. Got killed at a concert. Knifed."

"I am sure that you did everything you could for him."

"That's what our lass says." He wipes the top of the bottle with one oil-stained hand and offers it to me. "Come on. It's medicinal. Have one for Jake."

I take it from him – one hand keeps the towel in place – and lift the bottle to my lips. The alcohol warms me as Jake used to. He clumps back to the railings to finish his smoke.

Feeling bolder, I venture further.

"You're married then?"

"Nah. Girlfriend. She's married to a mate of mine."

"He won't be your friend long if he finds out about the two of you."

"He found out last weekend. Said he'd teach me a lesson." He shrugged. "I'm still waiting."

"What made you join the Hell's Angels?"

"What makes you ask that, Dorothy?"

No one has called me Dorothy in a long time. Usually, I get Dot, Grandma, or Mother. Only Jake called me Dorothy.

"Isn't that what it says on your jacket?"

He turned and fixed me with a scowl. Then his lips creased into a smile.

"Oh, that…"

He held up the jacket.

"Never could understand why someone would spoil a leather jacket by painting a woman's name on the back of it."

I could see then that the second 'A' had faded and that the letters spelled:

ANGELA and not ANGEL.

"Still, it were a bargain."

I felt relieved but a little foolish.

"You'd best get off now," he said. "You're a bad influence on me. Skinny-dippin', defacin' public property, drinkin' alcohol. Besides, our lass'll go mad."

"Why?"

He strides back to the bench and stands facing me, one hand resting on his hip, the other throwing the cigarette stub to the ground where it is crushed mercilessly under his heavy boot.

"She gets jealous when I'm courtin' other women."

I find this mildly amusing, as normally, I seem to be invisible to the younger generation.

I walk back to the car, pull on my clothes, and turn the key in the ignition. The engine starts and I turn the wheel to drive back up the road. I look in the rear-view mirror. He has left his jacket on the bench and is weaving back to the water's edge, one hand holds the whiskey bottle, and the other raises another hand-rolled cigarette to his lips.

It occurs to me then that I had not even asked for his name.

SPIRIT COVE MYSTERY

A stolen motorbike was found abandoned in Spirit Cove on Sunday afternoon. A brown leather jacket with the name 'Angela' painted on the back was found near the motorbike.

We are appealing to members of the public to contact us with any information that would help solve the mystery.

The Sandman

By Meg Fishburn

I always considered myself a country girl at heart. A life lived closer to the pulse of the earth, away from the fumes of the city, the incessant noise of close-packed humanity. My funds would hardly buy a country hut, let alone a rose-covered cottage.

When I agreed, with bad grace, to accompany a friend on a trip to a northern coastal village, I was expecting bleak, stony beaches and cold, biting winds. Stepping from the train, I viewed my surroundings. Sure, the overcast sky reflected grey on the water, but to my right, open fields stretched into the distance. Patches of woodland meandered carelessly across the landscape. Armed with the inevitable fish and chips, we set off to discover the beach. As we wandered through the dunes, the sun peeped through, casting a golden glow on the sandy shore.

I had found my utopia!

*

I look around at my house – a humble semi but with a garage and yes – a garden! How peaceful to watch the late sunset over the quiet fields. So many more stars to see without the intrusive streetlights. At the end of the long garden is a pond, overgrown but home to frogs and toads, whose amorous rumblings bemused me at first. Harvey, my dog, would career after the birds who flocked to my feeders.

There is a copse just below my house, through which runs the path to the beach. Harvey loved this track, pulling impatiently on his lead as I lagged behind.

On the beach I would walk to the right, the quieter route leading towards the neighbouring village. Left would take me to my noisier neighbour – a typical seaside town of takeaways and amusements. I was not keen on the town, but as spring drifted into early summer, I found myself wandering that way. On the approach is a small grassy park, almost adjoining the dunes.

Every year, there is an influx of sand artists, who with a mixture of permanent sand and imagination, create a tableau of exotic sculptures. This summer, there seemed to be a theme.

A fantastical castle, a splendour of spires and turrets. Statuesque Queen Boudicca, driving her carriage. I noticed a low bier and wandered over for closer inspection. The figure of a medieval king lay on it, sword at his side and crown placed upon his breast. Something caught my eye and I turned sharply – towering above me and hitherto unnoticed, was a dragon. Wings unfurled, sea glass eyes turned reverently towards its dead lord.

Through the summer I took my early walks along to the park, watching the formless sands take on a life of their own.

Early midsummer's eve, I strolled to the park with Harvey running ahead, barking joyously. He was always excitable at this time of year.

"All right, Harvey!"

I stopped in astonishment. "Don't remember seeing that yesterday!"

While the king slept peacefully and the dragon kept vigil, another figure appeared. Kneeling at the bier, head bent, the figure appeared to be dressed in rough sackcloth, arm resting on the hilt of a dagger.

Engrossed in my examination of the grizzled features, my reverie was broken by the sound of gushing liquid.

"Oh no, Harvey, not there!"

Harvey had relieved himself on the bier, some liquid splashing up onto the king's face, giving the appearance of tears flowing down his cheeks.

"Oh, Harvey, come away!"

Who can sleep on midsummer's eve? This year seemed idyllic, watching the sun set into the sea while Harvey embraced the scents of the garden. I pulled my lounger into the open doorway to gaze at the silvered sky. A large shadow crossed the moon, and I tried to recall the birds I'd seen in the wetlands – none so large as this, I thought drowsily.

I awoke suddenly to the sound of frantic yelping.

"Harvey?"

Only silence. Grabbing a torch, I cast the light around the garden. No Harvey, but an open garden gate. Cursing myself, I ran out, frantically calling for my beloved dog. There was only silence. As the sky lightened, my neighbour, Doug, joined the search.

He frowned. "What is all this sand doing in your garden?"

Trailing through the garden was a set of huge, sandy footprints.
"They are leading to the beach path."

We followed the track down to the beach, though in my heart, I knew it was hopeless – someone had taken Harvey.

"I'll go off to the right," Doug decided. "You head towards town."

*

No one had seen my beautiful dog; by the time I reached the park, I had given up hope. Aimlessly looking around, I frowned. Something was different. The king lay on his bier; the dragon, wings tightly furled, kept watch. Then I saw it – the kneeling figure had disappeared. No pile of sand to show it had ever been there. Just a row of huge, sandy footprints leading down through the dunes.

*

The packing boxes are ready to go, and the removal van is booked for nine. I am heading back to the city where the only creatures to be scared of are humans.

I sit on the dunes and watch the sun dipping into the sea, and I wonder.

How can something so beautifully tranquil conceal such seething rage?

That Date

By Roger Elgood

The headmaster arranged his papers on the highly-polished oak Thompson table before him and looked down on the sea of excited young female faces below.

It was the last morning of the Lent term, and this was the final assembly.

He reflected. Naturally, they were excited. The date hadn't helped. He had tried to avoid closing the school for the holidays on this particular morning, but circumstances had made it impossible. Friday was the traditional day on which to end the term, and there it was.

The morning hadn't passed off too badly, he mused. One or two of the sillier pupils had needed reminding of what behaviour was and was not acceptable, but nobody had overstepped the mark too badly, and in a very few moments, it would all be over until the next term.

Checking his notes, he started on the usual reminders, the clearing of the classrooms, collection of lost property, and the reminder that news of misbehaviour on the coaches would ultimately be passed back to him and retribution, albeit delayed, would follow. Then, suddenly, a thought struck him.

He had reached the final item on his list. Custom dictated that he should now wish pupils and staff a happy holiday and close the proceedings, but he paused.

The buzz of excitement in the hall died away, and the faces of staff and pupils alike turned toward him with renewed curiosity. This was something unexpected.

Measuring his words carefully and speaking even more clearly than usual, he commenced his pronouncement.

"You will all remember that, in February, we had to close the school for a day because of heavy snow.

"Just before assembly, I received a telephone call from the chairman, reminding me that we had lost a day's school and informing me that this day must be made up.

"I have to tell you, therefore, that notwithstanding the list of term dates published at the beginning of this academic year, the next

98

term will begin one day early."

The silence in the room was palpable. The faces of one or two staff members registered thinly-disguised mutiny. Incredulity, shock, and disappointment vied for supremacy.

The headmaster collected his notes, paused to make sure that his last announcement had made full effect, walked purposefully to the steps, and began to descend.

Halfway down he paused and turned to the assembled company.

"April Fools, the lot of you," he said.

How To Make A Man

By Anita Langham

Men are like early chess pieces – lumps of wood with few features, functional, useful even, but not aesthetically pleasing.

In the same way, a mother bear was believed to lick her cubs into shape, your man will need working on. This process is exactly like wood carving.

Having selected your block of wood with care, you need to sleep with it for a spell. During this time it'll reveal its intrinsic nature, its very soul, what it wants to be, and what it's capable of becoming. Once you understand this, apply your chisels to the whetting stone till they're sharp as an owl's flight feather, then, and only then, can you set to work.

Never carve across the grain, this runs the risk of weaker, more delicate parts snapping off. No, no, go *with* the grain – that way, your wood will carve like butter.

It'll take time, try your patience, exhaust you physically, mentally, and emotionally, but chip away at it, and one day, like the artists who fashioned their stained glass windows one piece at a time, you'll stand back, look up at the finished work and think: 'How beautiful is that?'

Borealis

By Jean Devasagyam

My grandfather's favourite quotation was, 'What is this life so full of care we have no time to stand and stare.' I wanted to encapsulate those times in Saltburn when I had stopped to just enjoy an inspiring moment – a sort of photo album of memories.

One, in particular, was very special. Sometimes you get a feeling something magical will happen, and just now and again, it really does.

I then set it to music as a song and first performed it at a folk workshop weekend run by Maddy Prior (of Steeleye Span fame) in Brampton. Maddy complimented me on the song and said I should keep it in my repertoire.

Slate grey ship silhouettes float on a shell-pink sea;
under soft sunset skies.
Drowsily turning waves enfold the land;
Hushing the swifts' shrill cries.
Afterglow fades to indigo
And now the sea sheens silver.
A moth feeds among the blooms;
Its mottled wings aquiver.
A pale, slender, crescent moon
Is underlined by a meteor's brief flight.
Bats flit along the grove
And rise to greet another new night.
Along the north horizon,
beyond the lighthouse gleaming,
In shifting veils of light and drifting hemline
seeming
With emeralds, pearls, and rubies sewn;
Aurora dances, Aurora dances, Aurora Borealis dances.

One Single Punch

By Jean Devasagyum

There is an epidemic going on in this country. No one can quite explain how it began nor when it will end. It proves life-changing for all affected and consumes precious NHS and Emergency Services resources. I wrote this poem in protest.

He entered, quietly, at the door,
With downcast eyes crossed the floor,
Sat on the chair beside the table,
Softly said, "I'll tell all I'm able."
Questions came then, thick and fast;
Name, age, job, and all his past.
Did he not know it wasn't right;
Being in a brawl the other night?
"Oh, I wasn't in it at the start;
Just passing by, quite apart.
The first lad shouted 'No, that's not right'.
It was the other lad who began the fight.
I felt I had to take a stand
When I saw the knife held in his hand.

He lashed out with lightning speed.
I saw the first lad wince and bleed.
"I used just, one, single, punch." he said,
"The knifer tumbled, hit his head
Upon the kerb; and lay there, dead."

'Touché'

By Pat Atkinson

"You're good, there's not much more I can teach you."

"Martin, you know I don't think of this as a lesson. It's war."

"War indeed is it, and I suppose you think you're the victor."

"Victrix Martin, victrix. I see you with every jab and stab as the perfect foil to a day with those pompous prigs in the boardroom."

"En-garde," she cried, advancing into assault. Forward and back, they encircled each other with enticing feints, then full of emotion their bodies corp-a-corp, they glanced tantalisingly into each other's eyes. Back and forth they went until with a powerful lunge, she made contact. "Touché," she cried.

Showered and exhilarated she asked Martin to join her for a meal at her favourite sushi bar in town.

"You are full of surprises," he said staring into her wolf-grey eyes, "I want to get to know you better."

"Hey, let's not rush into anything. Besides I'm a pussycat really, what you've seen so far is only a facade."

"Yeah, but I can see you're quite challenging. You like to set the pace, but need your own space."

"You've got me. I confess, but when two solar powers come together, amazing things happen."

Deep down she was overjoyed, she had taken charge and steered herself right into his heart. Martin was her ideal man.

After a brilliant weekend with Martin, she was supercharged and ready to take on any challenges that came her way. She took a deep breath, raised her head, and with a confident air, mouthed the words, 'En-garde', as she pushed open the boardroom door. Her campaign had reached its final offensive. Higgins and Hodgkins were toppled like dominoes, Salvatore and Haigh-Green surprisingly rallied to her cause without opposition. Bringloe and Parsons mounted a strong counter-attack. She must stay focused. Her goal was in sight, and she was aware that a late attack from them, the notorious fifth-column approach, could prove disastrous. As the day progressed she forged ahead unstoppable. She would control the company by nightfall having ousted the despicable Nigel Foster.

The next day as she woke she blinked slowly and deeply. It was not only a new dawn but a new beginning for her too. She felt good, a weight had been lifted from her shoulders, and yet the weight of responsibility she had fought for yesterday, in gaining control of the company, would challenge her greatly, but in a different way.

Her father had gone to his grave resolved to disappointment that the company his father had built up had slipped further and further from its roots. A twist of fate, ten years ago, when he was vulnerable through illness, had seen his nephew Nigel take control. Dominique could now fulfil his wishes having deposed the inscrutable relative. She would honour the principles of her father while adding her steely determination to succeed.

Returning to the piste that evening she felt her spent batteries were in need of recharging. "En-garde," she shouted with conviction as she and Martin advanced towards each other once more.

Grandma's Visit

By Pat Atkinson

On the day that my grandmother was arriving for a holiday with us, Mum was a bit on edge.

"Now listen, I want the day to go smoothly, I want Grandma to see that we can look organised, that we are a normal family. I don't want any mishaps or excuses I want everyone to sit down to an evening meal together. Josh, that means you too, don't drift off with your friends after school, come straight home. Libby, you too."

"Oh, Liz! I'm sorry, I have a date for the gym."

Mum thought Dad was serious until he added, "With my new personal trainer, the shapely Fiona Flinch."

Her long hard stare however showed her contempt and that it meant a lot to her for us to display a united front for Dad's mother's benefit. Her usual humour was non-existent until Dad smiled and she realised he was joking, but she still thrashed him playfully with the nearest thing to hand.

"Hey! Be careful, that folder contains my drawing for the B1229 prototype. Our ticket to fame and fortune, that is, if I can convince the panel that my calculations are sound."

She kissed him on the cheek. "Go," she said dramatically. "Take your scribbles with you. Go forth, Einstein, my mathematician husband."

Grandma was so proud of Dad. "He's very clever," she would say. Then would add sarcastically, "Pity neither you nor Josh have inherited his brains. You both must take after your mother."

I don't know if Mum ever heard Grandma's put-downs. She probably said them when she was out of the room, but something made Mum edgy whenever she was coming to stay. She just wanted us to be on our best behaviour and we tried, honestly, we did try.

As soon as the breakfast lecture concluded we left to begin our day, Dad to aerospace, Josh and I to Macmillan Academy and Mum to her brood of little chick chicks as she called her charges at Nursery School.

At the sound of the last bell of the day, I made my way out to the school grounds only to be turned back by a burly policeman. "There's been an incident. Go back into school for your safety."

Staff were now swarming out of the main entrance to reunite us with our form teachers. I caught sight of Josh. He held up his hand as clueless as the rest of us. Mum won't believe it's not our fault that we're going to be late. Dad will calm her down. She's so reliant on him, still, she would never admit it.

The deafening chitter chatter in our form room was brought to a stunned silence as Miss Rayson gave details that an armed robber had stormed one of the banks on the High Street.

"Your parents are being informed, but until the police say it's safe, you are to remain here."

My pleas that our grandma is arriving for a visit today, that she will be out there somewhere in the held-up traffic, didn't allow me special leave, and I reluctantly take my seat alongside my classmates. The loudest loudmouth in Year 10 started to wind everyone up saying, "The cops will never catch'em, they're useless, the robbers will come to hide in school, and we'll all be killed." Her attempt to frighten us resulted in her becoming hysterical and Miss Rayson asking me to take her to Mrs Cresor's first aid room. That done I made my escape, fled from school by the back gate which was actually out of bounds to us, but these are exceptional circumstances as Grandma must see that we are just so very sensible and caring.

I caught up with Josh as he bounded over the wall having made his escape from the toilet block.

"Great minds think alike. So, Grandma is wrong," I say. "We must take after Dad. We must be clever."

"Oh! Come on," Josh said. "I don't care about all that stuff. I have to get home before anyone else does."

"Why? Are you hiding something?"

"Nothing that need concern you, but if Grandma has already arrived, will you keep her indoors while I …"

The sound of another siren cut in, and he clammed up. The front door is still locked so thankfully we have arrived home first. As I put my key into the lock Josh dashes through the side gate into the garden and full of curiosity, I follow. We stopped dead at the sight of two armed officers leaping over the back fence.

"Stand clear," they shout, "get back in the house." I stare in stunned silence as Josh shouts at them not to shoot and flings himself towards the shed door. One cop pushed Josh aside as they trained their weapons on the slowly opening creaky door, and out stumbled one dishevelled grandmother, one very angry goose, and five flustered fluffy goslings, but no sign of the armed robbers.

The officers retreat with stern promises to sort Josh out later.

"Grandma, nice to see you," I offer, whilst looking round at Josh in despair, desperate to know why he had a goose and her offspring in our garden shed.

Mum and Dad arrived home and Mum started to reel off a list of things she needed explaining. Grandma was given a 'stiff' drink, as Dad called it. "To steady your nerves."

He calmed the rest of us down by saying his design had been accepted. Josh and I were euphoric at Dad's good fortune, hoping the last hour's escapades were forgotten. However, he continued. "Tomorrow will be soon enough to face up to an inquest about today's misdemeanours."

"That's right!" Mum shrieked, almost reaching top C, "Your head might be full of numbers, calculations, formulae, but everything else, the trouble the children are in, for instance, is of no importance to you."

Dad put his arm around Mum's waist hesitantly in case she was going to spout on. "Tomorrow," he said calmly, "is another day."

"You are all mad. This is a mad house. No wonder I don't visit too often," Grandma shouted. But then her mood changed completely as she declared, "You, son, are so very clever. I'm proud of you."

Mum cut her short, "We're mad, we're mad, Millie," she scorned, "I have yet to learn what you were doing in our garden shed and why the police thought you were the armed robber?" Josh made for the doorway with Mum's voice ringing in his ears. "And you, yes you, Josh, want to tell us anything about goosey, goosey gander?"

Tears of the Sloth

By Anita Langham

Enemies, sweethearts, and sins in the world of a sloth moth, (*Cryptoses choloepi*), a *3-toed Sloth* (*Bradypus variegatus infuscatus*) and the disappearing rain forests of the Amazon Basin.

Brown and stripy, a little snout moth
I'm living in the fur of a three-toed Sloth,
Who hangs in the canopy upside down,
With curving claws and face of a clown.
I evolved just for her, yet I have to share,
There's an ecosystem living in her hair,
Of flies and fungi, mosquitoes and mites,
Blood-sucking flies and fat white lice.
In a forest of algae, lichens and bacteria,
I kiss away secretions, drink each tear.
It's a living model of mutuality though,
I fertilise her algae with nitrogen and so
Her fur goes green, and that transition
Helps with her camouflage and nutrition.
Once a week, when Sloth clambers down
To visit her midden heap on the ground,
I leave that haven to which I'd clung,
And deposit my eggs on her nice fresh dung.
Then when my larvae morph into moths,
They fly up to find their own dear sloths.
It's a perfect arrangement as you can see,
We're happy sweethearts, Sloth and me,
Except for the deadliest enemy we've got,
Not harpy eagle, jaguar, not even ocelot,
It's what we hear when the loggers appear,
The power saw's whine is what we fear,
When Sloth meets, to our consternation,
Old Avarice in the guise of de-forestation.

Memories of Anne Gibbons

By Karin Slade

A little serendipity came at the end of Anne's life when she had to enter a care home; several of the staff in the care home had been trained by Anne, and this helped her settle as she often thought she was back at work.

*****

Haiku
Anita Langham

Female dotterels
practised free love long before
women's lib was born

Mother's Rembrandt

By Anita Langham

That was the year a television show featuring lost masterpieces coincided with an advert in the *Yorkshire Post* for an antiques auction at our local saleroom. A trawl through the internet and a quantum leap later, Mother announced that the gloomy old painting on our landing was definitely a Rembrandt. She'd bought it at an Antiques & Collectibles because she liked the subject, though seeing she didn't even like her own kids, a woman bending over a crib seemed a strange choice. But, you humoured our mother or were cast into outer darkness forever, so I shrugged.

"Crack on, go for it."

Out came the Fairy Liquid and sponge pads. Years of grime and fag-smoke gurgled down the plughole. Out sprang motes of dust suspended in the sunbeam that flooded in through the leaded window. That cast a bright oblong across a framed map and the portrait of a young man. Highlighted a finial on the panelled crib, the contours of the woman's white collar glistened on her heartbreak curls. So still, so tranquil. Hang about. This shit might well be true after all.

"Have you been cleaning this?" enquired the guest expert suspiciously.

Guilt flickered across Mother's face like harvest lightning. "*No!*"

"Really? In any case, that's no Rembrandt. Everything about it's wrong."

Instant humiliation. I rolled my eyes. Turned away.

"However," the expert added, "if I'm not very much mistaken, this painting's about to rock the art world. I think it could be the only Vermeer self-portrait ever found…"

On Hearing That Giraffes Can't Swim

By Anita Langham

As light shimmers hazily,
You float lazily
And breeze adzes facets
Over the sea,
Then cast by refraction,
Sun makes mosaics,
Paints giraffe patterns on
Your arms and legs,
So limbs hair and seagrass
Swirl drift and mingle
With the motion of a
Turquoise ocean

Acknowledgements

Haikus:
Haikus throughout the anthology written by Anita Langham

Photographs:

Anne in her nest – Maggie Gibbons
Anne in front of the mosaics opposite Saltburn Station –
Karin Slade
Rexel – By kind permission of Roger Elgood
The Giant Racer – Supplied by Norma Cuthbert

Additional information supplied by Jim Gibbons

Printed in Great Britain
by Amazon

32448002R00066